W9-CCQ-518

Dear Reader,

We're delighted to bring you Helen Brooks's fortieth romance! *Sleeping Partners* is a wonderful story, brimming with passion and emotion…and we hope you'll enjoy the sparkle and intensity that Helen always brings to her characters.

Helen Brooks is especially popular for the gorgeous, strong and dynamic heroes she creates. Always commanding, always highly sensual—and always tamed at last by a warm and spirited heroine!

A natural storyteller, Helen keeps readers around the world frantically turning the pages of her books. She creates emotional journeys for her characters with a powerful depth of feeling—with a few tears and plenty of smiles along the way.

Congratulations on your fortieth Harlequin romance, Helen!

With best wishes
The Editors

NINE TO FIVE

*Getting down to business
in the boardroom...and the bedroom!*

A secret romance, a forbidden affair,
a thrilling attraction...

What happens when two people work together
and simply can't help falling in love—
no matter how hard they try to resist?

Find out in this series of stories
set against working backgrounds.

This month it's
Sleeping Partners by Helen Brooks

Look out for

Back in the Boss's Bed by Sharon Kendrick
on sale in Harlequin Presents in May, #2322

Helen Brooks

SLEEPING PARTNERS

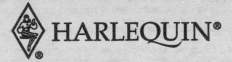

TORONTO • NEW YORK • LONDON
AMSTERDAM • PARIS • SYDNEY • HAMBURG
STOCKHOLM • ATHENS • TOKYO • MILAN • MADRID
PRAGUE • WARSAW • BUDAPEST • AUCKLAND

If you purchased this book without a cover you should be aware
that this book is stolen property. It was reported as "unsold and
destroyed" to the publisher, and neither the author nor the
publisher has received any payment for this "stripped book."

ISBN 0-373-12310-8

SLEEPING PARTNERS

First North American Publication 2003.

Copyright © 2001 by Helen Brooks.

All rights reserved. Except for use in any review, the reproduction or
utilization of this work in whole or in part in any form by any electronic,
mechanical or other means, now known or hereafter invented, including
xerography, photocopying and recording, or in any information storage
or retrieval system, is forbidden without the written permission of the
publisher, Harlequin Enterprises Limited, 225 Duncan Mill Road,
Don Mills, Ontario, Canada M3B 3K9.

All characters in this book have no existence outside the imagination of
the author and have no relation whatsoever to anyone bearing the same
name or names. They are not even distantly inspired by any individual
known or unknown to the author, and all incidents are pure invention.

This edition published by arrangement with Harlequin Books S.A.

® and TM are trademarks of the publisher. Trademarks indicated with
® are registered in the United States Patent and Trademark Office, the
Canadian Trade Marks Office and in other countries.

Visit us at www.eHarlequin.com

Printed in U.S.A.

CHAPTER ONE

'CLAY LINCOLN! Are you mad, Cassie?' Robyn's beautiful velvet-brown eyes were narrowed with disgust. 'I'd rather walk through the streets of London stark naked than ask Clay Lincoln for help.'

'You wouldn't be asking him for help though.' Cassie Barnes's voice was as impassive as her face. 'You would merely be giving him the chance to buy into a thriving little concern that will eventually net him a considerable profit.'

'Whatever.'

'He's ridiculously well off, Robyn.'

'So?' It was truculent.

'So...' Cassie sighed patiently, her role of elder sister by five years very evident by the maternal streak in her voice '...you need a backer if you're going to take your business onto the next stage, and everyone else you've approached is either flat broke or simply not interested, your bank manager included. Clay seems the perfect solution to me.'

'Clay Lincoln is not a perfect anything!' The bitterness was acidic. 'And frankly I'd rather stay as a one-man band for the rest of my life than have anything to do with that low life.'

'No, you wouldn't.' Cassie looked at the lovely heart-shaped face in front of her which at the moment was flushed a defiant red, the colour indicative of the hot temper that went with the clouds of burnished red-gold curls tied high on Robyn's head. She sighed again, this time silently. Robyn had inherited all of their mother's volatile, fiery nature and none of their father's placid equability.

'You know you wouldn't,' she said again. 'You're ambitious and incredibly talented and good at what you do, and you've worked your socks off to get where you are right now. How many other women of twenty-eight have their own PR company? And you'll go places, I know you will. You *deserve* success, Robyn.'

Robyn looked at her sister's sweetly earnest face and the dark shadows beneath Cassie's mild hazel eyes—courtesy of the fact that she had been up half the night with her twin boys which didn't sit well with being five months pregnant—and felt instant contrition. 'Oh, I'm sorry, Cass, I am really. I'm being a pig and I know you mean it for the best but I couldn't approach Clay Lincoln for all the tea in China.'

'Well, Guy still sees him occasionally; I'm sure he would—'

'Cassie, *no*!' Robyn interrupted vehemently.

'All right, all right.' Cassie held up her hands in defeat. 'Whatever you say, Robyn.'

'I'll expand in time and for the moment Drew is happy to work all the hours under the sun. She's just thrown the latest live-in boyfriend out 'cos he was messing around, and she's off men.'

'Until the next one arrives,' Cassie said darkly. She disapproved of Robyn's assistant's somewhat promiscuous lifestyle from her matronly position of being married for twelve years to Guy Barnes, her first boyfriend whom she had met when she had been sixteen and had married five years later.

'As you say, until the next one arrives.' Robyn laughed in agreement. If she was to speak truthfully she would have to admit to a sneaking admiration for Drew. She had known the tall, leggy blonde since they had done a post-graduate diploma in public and media relations together, and in all that time—seven years now—Drew's torrid love life and penchant for picking the worst rats in society had never got the other woman down. After each disastrous affair Drew would have a little cry, declare she was going to devote herself exclusively to her career, her cats and her friends—usually in that order—and blow her current bank balance on designer outfits to cheer herself up. The longest the celibate state had lasted had been one month some years ago, and that had only been because Drew had had a severe attack of a particularly nasty flu and had been in bed for two weeks.

'Robyn, most days you're in your office before eight a.m. and you don't get home until eight or nine; later when there's a launch party of something. When do you ever *relax*?' Cassie said worriedly.

'It's not as bad as that.'

'It's worse,' Cassie said plaintively. 'You never get the chance to meet anyone.'

'Cass, I meet people all the time,' Robyn said firmly, knowing where this conversation was going to lead. It was the same one they had had many times in the past and it never varied in its content.

'You know what I mean.' Cassie had got the bit between her teeth, her freckles all but popping off her face in protest. 'The last time you went out on a date was *months* ago. All work and no play—'

'Makes this lady a fulfilled and happy one,' Robyn interrupted with a grin at her sister's disgruntled face. 'I like my life the way it is, Cass.' And at her sibling's snort of despair, she added, 'I *do*. You know I've never been one for serious relationships, Cass. It's not my style.'

'No relationships at all is your style,' Cassie retorted promptly.

'Perhaps, but that's me. You chose Guy and kids and domesticity; I chose career.' Robyn was trying very hard to keep it friendly and calm but it was hard. Since their parents had moved to a retirement bungalow in the south of France Cassie had taken on the role of bossy and protective older sister with a vengeance. She meant well, Robyn reminded herself, and there wasn't a malicious or nasty bone in Cassie's whole body, but she did go on at times!

'But having a career doesn't cut out meeting Mr Right,' Cassie began fervently, only to stop and lift her head as she added, 'That's Guy and the kids home, and just when we were having such a good chat.'

'Pity,' Robyn agreed drily, noting with a pang of guilt that the sarcasm went completely over Cassie's head.

At least Guy's return from his Sunday afternoon visit to the park with the twins focused Cassie's attention on tea and baths for her exuberant offspring, but once Robyn was on her way home to her little flat above the office of her PR business in Kensington later that evening, she found her thoughts returning to the conversation with her sister, or to one particular part of it anyway.

Clay Lincoln. If she shut her eyes—which would be very dangerous considering she was driving her little blue Fiesta—she could see him as clearly as anything. Black hair, ice-blue eyes and a smile to die for—or so she had thought once, she corrected herself swiftly. Twelve years ago to be exact, when she had been a very young and silly sixteen and he had been a devastingly experienced twenty-three.

He had been at university with Guy and so had briefly been part of her sister and brother-in-law's circle. She had idolised him from afar as a spotty adolescent just going into her teens when Clay had spent time with Guy and his friends in the university recesses. If he'd deigned to speak to her at all it had been with the sort of indulgent kindness most adults applied to children.

And then her spots had cleared up and she had had the brace off her teeth and had learnt how to manage her riotous mass of curly hair, just in time to be Cassie and Guy's bridesmaid when her sister had got married.

Her stomach turned over and she breathed deeply, willing the memories back under lock and key. It worked usually; she kept the little box in her mind labelled Clay Lincoln closed at all times having learnt from past experience that she only had to relax her guard for a while and the lid flew open, regurgitating all the pain and humiliation. Tonight, though, seemed to be an exception.

She brought the car to a halt at some traffic lights and opened the window while she waited for the lights to change, breathing deeply again of the mild June air which was laden with the peculiarly distinct smell of the city.

It had all happened so long ago, she told herself firmly. She had been a different person then, coping with rampaging hormones and tumultuous emotions under the fragile exterior of burgeoning womanhood. Being tall and slender she had looked older than her sixteen years but the childish heroworship with which she had adored Clay had been there still under the surface. And she had been so thrilled, so elated when she had looked at herself in her bridesmaid finery and seen a slim young woman who had looked every day of twenty or so. After the years of spots and braces it had gone to her head.

She shut her eyes tightly, gripping the steering wheel with knuckles that turned white. She had played with fire, manipulated it even, and she had been badly burnt. It had been her own fault, all of it, but the resulting scars were still tender and had shaped the person she was today in a way she could never have imagined that summer's day so long ago.

As an irate horn behind her brought her eyes snapping open she saw the lights were green and in her hurry she stalled the engine, causing the car behind her to emit another loud blast.

Damn! Her cheeks were scarlet by the time she moved off. She hadn't stalled a car in years and it was all the more galling that it had happened through thinking about Clay Lincoln! How could just *thinking* about him reduce her to a flustered sixteen-year-old schoolgirl instead of the cool, sophisticated woman of the world she now purported to be?

She bit her lip hard, angry with herself and the world in general and especially Clay Lincoln. Ruthless ice man that he had been. She repeated the thought for extra emphasis before she determined to put Clay back where he belonged: in the box in her mind with his name on it and with the words, The past—dead and buried, in great red letters beside it.

It was just beginning to spot with rain when she drew up outside the narrow, terraced, three-story property she had purchased five years before, courtesy of an inheritance left by her maternal grandmother. Her mother had been an only child but after Robyn's grandfather had died her parents had made it plain they preferred any inheritance to be split between their two daughters rather than having anything themselves.

Consequently both Robyn and Cassie had been the sole recipients of their grandmother's estate, which had afforded the two women a very nice nest egg of some one hundred and fifty thousand pounds each. Cassie had been planning to start a family and she and Guy had decided to keep a portion of their windfall for all the expenses that would entail, just buying an estate car and banking the remainder of the money. But Robyn had put every penny of her hundred and fifty thousand pounds into buying her first home which had mean her mortgage was gratifyingly small.

The house had been well-maintained but was dark and gloomy, and so she'd ploughed much of the salary she'd earned working as a PR assistant for a record company into it over the next two years, always with a view to the future. And the future had meant her own PR firm, which she had achieved with Drew as her assistant just as Cassie had finally fallen with the twins after two years of trying.

The ground floor of the house was one long open-plan office, the floor above, Robyn's bathroom and kitchen, and the top floor her living quarters which again was one long room with a bedroom area at one end. She had painted this room in pale buttery yellow and had sanded and varnished the floorboards. Due to it being south-facing the new colour scheme drank in every ray of sunshine which was reflected in the warm-ochre bed-settee, pine table and chairs and the floating brick-red viole drapes at the French windows which led onto the minute balcony. It was radiant and cheerful and Robyn loved it; she loved the whole house, along with the work she did. Life was good.

She nodded to the thought as she opened the front door and stepped inside out of the drizzle. Yes, life was good. The last three years had seen an increase in clients which had surprised and delighted her, mainly because she was passionate about her work and right from the beginning had had the courage to only get involved in products she truly believed in. Journalists were canny folk: they could always see straight through any dissimulation.

Without pausing downstairs she climbed the stairs—again varnished and devoid of carpet—to the bathroom, where she began to run a bath before making herself a cup of hot chocolate in her bright streamlined kitchen. Once undressed and in her thick towelling robe she carried the hot chocolate through to the bathroom, setting it on the floor at the side of the bath before she sank into the silky bubbles.

If only her bank manager had been more positive about the business loan she'd applied for... She drained the mug and leant her head back against the smooth surface of the big cast-iron bath the house had boasted when she'd bought it, and which she had had resurfaced in gleaming white. She desperately needed a second assistant; Cassie had been right this afternoon in that the workload was becoming too much. But only in that! All that talk about Clay Lincoln had been crazy.

Her eyes closed as the caressing warmth of the hot water did its work on tired muscles, and before she could stop it, her mind had taken her back in time to Cassie's wedding day. As bridesmaid, she'd been dressed in a gorgeous dress of pale jade silk, her curls threaded with tiny, fresh white orchids and her face alight with the wonder of being sixteen and desirable. Or at least she had imagined she was desirable.

She shifted in the water, but it was too late. She was sixteen again: young, vulnerable and breathtakingly in love with life. With life and Clay Lincoln. He had been so handsome that her knees had turned to jelly every time she'd seen him and on this day, Cassie and Guy's wedding day, he had looked like a Hollywood film star. Better than a Hollywood film star. The smart suit and silver-blue shirt and tie which had exactly matched the devastatingly cool eyes had held her transfixed.

And he had noticed her. For the first time he had noticed her. She had seen something in his eyes when she had followed the bridal pair down the aisle, her arm in that of Guy's married brother who had been the best man. She couldn't have found words to describe what she'd seen, she'd just known that in the three years before that day it had not been there.

It had made her want to shout and dance, to act crazy, but instead she had stood outside the church posing for pictures as though the only thing on her mind was the success of Cassie's special day.

Clay had stood at the back of the crowd, his dark good looks brooding, but she'd been aware of every little movement he had made. The minute he had turned his head, whom he had spoken to, how many times he had smiled or nodded—her mind had recorded it all, along with the breadth of his strong shoulders, the magnetic pull of his overwhelming masculinity.

The reception had been typical of such occasions, she supposed. Feverish gaiety, endless speeches, toasts and more toasts, but all she had known was that when the dancing had started Clay had danced with everyone but her.

It had hurt. Desperately, tragically, in a way that only sixteen-year olds can feel, and towards the end of the evening she had passed through every emotion known to man.

The reception had been held at a lavish hotel overlooking a vast, man-made lake, and just before ten o'clock she had noticed Clay walk out of the big open doors at the end of the room and disappear into the shadows beyond. Even now she didn't know what had made her follow him.

Curiosity, desire, frustration, desperation, love... Probably a mixture of all of them.

The sky had been a deep indigo velvet pierced with stars, flooded with an ethereal whispering stillness that had made the scented air rich and heavy. It had been intoxicating.

He had been standing at the edge of the lake some distance from the lighted hotel, his dark bulk silhouetted against the water, and he hadn't been aware of her presence until she had almost reached him. She'd gazed at him, *aching* with love.

'Robyn?' He turned as she trod on a small twig which alerted him to the fact that she was there. And then the look of bemusement changed and he said, his voice forced and teasing in a way she found insulting, 'What are you doing out here? You'll spoil that pretty dress of yours if you aren't careful,' as though she was six years old instead of sixteen.

'It's hot in there.' She continued to his side, her stomach churning with her temerity. She paused, and then summoned every ounce of courage she possessed and said, her voice quiet and her eyes wide and serious, 'Why didn't you want to dance with me, Clay?'

'Dance with you?' He cleared his throat before smiling carefully, but she noticed it didn't reach the silver blue of his eyes. 'You're in such demand tonight no one can get near you.' His voice with its faint American accent was overhearty.

'That's not true.' She didn't know what was driving her but the night was timeless and enchanting and she had loved him so much for so long, and then to be disappointed afresh...

'No?' He opened his mouth to make some light, throwaway remark—she saw it in his face—but then as his eyes met hers he froze and it seemed as though they both stopped breathing. 'Robyn...'

'What?' She moved even closer, her heart thundering at the look on his face. She might never get a chance like this again.

'This is madness.' It was a husky murmur, almost a sigh. 'You're a baby.'

'I'm not a baby.' She was hardly aware of reaching up to put her arms round his neck, her body pliant as the delicious smell of him wrapped round her. She'd show him she wasn't a baby.

Slowly and very gently his arms pulled her against the hard solid wall of his chest, and as his face had come nearer she waited for the kiss in a rush of excitement that was too intense to bear. The taste and the feel of him was spinning in her head as his lips met hers, and as she gave a little moan of longing he answered it with a harsh, guttural sound of his own, his mouth becoming urgent and hungry.

At first she felt a slight sense of shock, the tiniest recoil as his tongue moved probingly against her lips, but almost immediately it was replaced with waves of delight as sensation after sensation began to bring her tinglingly alive.

Her body was moulded against his now, the vital male smell of him filling her nostrils and the alien sense of his hidden power and dominance becoming real as the thrust of his body against hers proclaimed his arousal. How long they continued to kiss she didn't know, but their bodies were so close she could feel his heart slamming against his ribcage and feel every small tremor as his mouth left hers to blaze a burning trail down her throat and into the soft swell of her breasts.

He tried to move away at one point, his voice hoarse

as he said, 'We have to stop, Robyn, now. You're Cassie's little sister for crying out loud...'

But she pulled his head down to hers in answer, her love for him taking precedence over anything else and her surrender complete. His kisses and caresses were better than her most erotic dreams and she knew—she *knew*—she would never love anyone but Clay. She was moving mindlessly against him as he kissed her with a hungry intensity that was thrilling, his hands exploring her soft curves and causing her to arch and twist.

Her dress was off her shoulders now, exposing the pure creamy skin enhanced provocatively by the special lacy strapless bra she had bought. Then that too was peeled away from her hot skin and the full thrust of her breasts laid bare.

She should have felt shy; this was the first time she had even kissed a boy let alone been caressed and touched like this, but she felt nothing but elation and a wish to be even nearer to him as first his hands and then his lips made her arch with pleasure. This was Clay, she had dreamed of this moment, tasted it.

What would have happened if her name hadn't been called into the dark shadows in which they were enclosed, she didn't know. Or then again she did, only too well...

Robyn twisted jerkily in the bath, a wave of water slopping perilously close to the edge as the memories became almost too painful to contemplate.

Cassie and Guy had been ready to leave the reception and she had been missed. As their bridesmaid she had to wave them off.

She had tried to ignore the searching voices but Clay had frozen at the first shout, his muscled chest clenching before his breath had been hissed out between his teeth as he had very firmly put her from him, drawing first her bra and then her dress into place with hands that had shook slightly.

She remembered she'd made a small sound of protest, her arms reaching out to him again, but he had stepped back a pace, his voice grim as he'd said, 'This should never have happened, Robyn. Hell, it must be the wine and the atmosphere and the fact that you're so different tonight. But you're too young, a child still, and I should never have touched you.'

'I'm not a child.' It hurt, terribly. 'I'm over sixteen.' She couldn't believe he'd called her a child again.

'Sixteen?' His laugh was harsh, like a bark. 'Damn it all, I'm twenty-three.' And he glared at her.

'I don't care.' The voices were still there in the background and she felt desperate to make him understand before they were found. 'I—I've loved you for ages.'

'Loved me?' The note in his voice cut her in two and it was in that moment she discovered that love and hate are different sides of the same coin. 'You're barely out of nappies for crying out loud. How can you know what love is?'

She stared at him, too devastated to say a thing, and he glared back at her as he continued, 'I don't know what you've been up to with boys at school but judging by tonight it's too damn much. I came very near to having you just now; do you understand that? Now, whether it'd be the first time or not for you is neither here or there, *I* know I should never have laid a finger on you. I've let Cassie and Guy down as well as myself.'

Cassie's voice rose above the other calls and on hearing it Robyn whirled round and away from him, skimming across the grass like a will o' the wisp, her hands pressed to her lips as she struggled not to cry. She paused to catch her breath before she emerged from the concealing shad-

ows into the lights of the massive patio outside the room
her parents had hired for the reception, adjusting her
clothes and smoothing her hair. Then, forcing a smile to
her face, she called, 'I'm here, Cass.'

'Where on earth have you been?'

It was her mother who spoke, her voice irritable, but
Robyn ignored her, running over to Cassie and Guy and
flinging her arms round her sister as she said brokenly,
'Oh, Cass, I'm going to miss you so much.'

'No, you won't! I'm only going to be a few minutes
away and you can come round whenever you like. And
think, Robyn, no more fights over the bathroom!' Cassie
said, her own voice husky.

Their hugs and kisses masked Robyn's shock and despair; everyone took her tears as emotion at Cassie having
married, knowing how close the two sisters were.

And then Guy's brother called that he'd brought the car
round to the front of the hotel and they all poured through
reception and out onto the drive. Guy's brother and cronies had done a good job on Guy's Cavalier, with shaving
foam, ribbons and a supermarket-load of tin cans, and
soon the happy couple were off in a hail of rice and con-
fetti and ribald shouts from Guy's football cronies, some
of which made her mother's face tighten.

Robyn stood stiff and still looking after the departing
lights of the car, willing herself not to give way to the
storm of emotion that was like a great hot ball in her chest.
She had to get through this with a modicum of dignity,
she told herself silently. No one, *no one* must guess what
had happened, not a hint. She wouldn't be able to bear it.
She wouldn't.

The whole episode hadn't been Clay's idea. *She* had
followed *him* out to the lake when he had made it perfectly clear all evening he didn't want to have anything

to do with her. She had thrown herself at him, quite literally—offered herself on a plate. No, not even offered, she corrected painfully—forced herself on him more like. She'd instigated everything, *everything*. What had possessed her? And now he thought she was loose, anybody's...

And then his voice sounded just behind her, saying coolly, 'Robyn, we need to talk.' His hand took her elbow, turning her to face him. His face was closed, inscrutable.

'Let go of me.' Her voice surprised her: she didn't expect it to be so firm or so cold considering what she was feeling like inside. 'Don't you dare touch me.'

He complied, instantly.

'I've nothing to say to you, Clay, beyond that I'm as sorry as you at what happened tonight,' she said tautly. 'So, can we leave it at that?' She stepped away from him as she spoke.

The other guests were moving back inside and her mother approached them, sniffling loudly as she gushed how *wonderful* Cassie had looked and how *desperately* they were going to miss her. Robyn took her mother's arm, making some light comment that she was quite proud of when her heart and her pride were in tatters, and once inside the hotel she slipped into the ladies' cloakroom, locking the door of one of the cubicles behind her. She stayed in there some time, sick and numb with agonising misery and shame, and when she emerged Clay had already left.

She discovered the next morning, listening to her parents chat over breakfast, that Clay had apparently had a plane to catch having pulled off some big deal in the States. Her father was full of it, declaring they had been lucky to see him at all considering the way Clay's particular star was rising in the world of business since his father had died.

'He'll go places, that young man,' Mr Brett stated firmly. 'He might have been born with something of a silver spoon in his mouth but he's not your average, spoilt rich kid, not Clay Lincoln. He'll go to the very top, you mark my words.'

Robyn knew exactly what Clay Lincoln was, and also the place she would like him to go. Shame and disillusionment and pain ate her up for months on end and she buried herself in working for her A levels, refusing all offers of dates from any young hopefuls and keeping herself strictly to herself.

Time passed. She gained first-class grades in her examinations and went to university with the wounds having healed to some extent. But she was wary, extremely wary, of the opposite sex. The odd date, a casual friend or two was fine; anything other than that and she wasn't interested. It wasn't that she purposely shut her mind and heart to love and commitment, more that it would take a special man to give her the confidence to become vulnerable again.

The special man hadn't come along, the years had passed, and now she was twenty-eight and liked her life the way it was.

She sat up suddenly in the bath, angry that she had so completely indulged herself with memories that were difficult even now to come to terms with. They said that time heals all wounds... Robyn grimaced to herself as she stepped out of the bath and wrapped a big fluffy towel round herself, sarong fashion. Maybe, in ninety-nine per cent of cases that was true, but where Clay Lincoln was concerned the scar tissue was almost raw. But that was her problem.

Her soft mouth tightened, and the chocolate brown eyes fringed by thick black lashes that drew so many male glances on a day-to-day basis lost their velvet warmth and became as hard as iron as they narrowed reflectively.

She had thrown herself at him that day so many years ago and had probably got exactly what she had deserved. She had come to terms with that years ago, but it had taught her a lesson about the ruthless, hard quality of the opposite sex she had never forgotten. He had made her feel less than the dirt under his shoes that night, and however stupid she had been—and she *had* been stupid all right—she still didn't think she'd deserved that. She'd only been sixteen for goodness' sake.

But it didn't matter. She walked through to the bedroom, sitting down at her small but exquisite dressing table that had been her grandmother's. She stared into the misty mirror at the large-eyed girl staring back at her, and nodded defiantly. No, it really didn't matter. Clay Lincoln was a figure from the past; it had been Cassie's talk of him that had triggered these reflections. He was in a different world from her now.

He had had the meteoric success in the business world her father had predicted, his star dazzling, and she had caught glimpses of it now and again in the newspapers and had heard reports from Cassie and Guy who still saw him very occasionally. But she had made sure their paths never crossed. It had been better for everyone that way.

She had known when he had got married in the States to an American girl a short time after that fateful night at the lake, and also when his wife had died some years later, but she never pursued a conversation about Clay Lincoln. She had told Cassie and Guy she didn't like him, pretending it was just that she found him abrupt and cold and that she disapproved of the playboy image he had adopted after the death of his wife. If Cassie had ever wondered at her animosity regarding Guy's old friend she had never said so.

Robyn breathed in deeply, reaching for the rich moisturising cream in front of her without taking her eyes off the ones staring back at her from the mirror.

She neither wanted nor needed to see Clay Lincoln again. Not ever. And nothing would ever make her change her mind on that point. And as for Cass's suggestion of approaching him with a view to him having a stake in her business, her own special baby—she would rather go bankrupt!

CHAPTER TWO

'ROBYN, you remember Clay Lincoln, don't you? Guy and Clay were at university together.'

Robyn had just stepped into Cassie's large open-plan lounge where her sister's dinner guests were gathered in celebration of Guy's thirty-fifth birthday. She had been smiling as she'd walked into the room but in the last moment the smile had been wiped off her face with shock. According to Cassie there had been three couples Robyn knew quite well invited to dinner tonight, along with Guy's brother whom Robyn was partnering due to Cassie's sister-in-law being away in Blackpool at a conference the bank she worked for had organised and which Beryl had been unable to get out of.

But the tall, lean man in front of her was definitely not dear old Jim. And the photos she had seen of Clay in the newspapers over the last years had failed to do him justice. Twelve years ago he had been pretty stupendous; now he was easily the most handsome man she had ever seen in spite of the jet-black hair she remembered now being liberally streaked with silver.

He was bigger—broader—than he had been at twenty-three but only in the breadth of his shoulders and chest; the leanness that had always given his good looks an almost animal quality was still there, but made all the more powerful by maturity.

The youthful face had changed into one in which cynicism had scored deep lines which annoyingly only heightened his attractiveness; the silver-blue eyes were piercing in the deeply tanned skin and his mouth was possessed of hard worldly sensuality she was sure had not been there twelve years ago.

It was a disturbing face, magnetic in quality but almost too male, even cruel. But why was his face—along with the rest of him—present in Cass's house tonight? Robyn took a deep, hidden breath, silently thanked the guardian angel who had prompted her to make a special effort to look her best tonight, and said carefully, 'Hello, Clay; it must have been years since I saw you last,' as though she wasn't aware of the exact date or circumstances.

'Yes, it must.' His voice was the same—dark, smoky— and it caught at her nerve endings making them tingle. 'Cassie and Guy's wedding I believe, so that's all of twelve years in a couple of months time,' he said easily.

'Really? That long?' How could Cass *do* this to her? Robyn was intensely, almost painfully, aware of the narrowed blue eyes taking in every detail of her appearance, but the expensive cream shot-silk chiffon dress and matching sandals, and the sparkling Cartier diamond studs in her ears which had been her twenty-first birthday present from her parents, more than stood up to the piercing scrunity. Which was a darn sight more than her legs felt able to do right at this moment!

She knew her face was flushed—she had always blushed easily, it went with the red hair and creamy skin—but there was nothing she could do about that and perhaps he wouldn't notice.

Clay, on the other hand, was as cool and contained as she remembered, his handsome, finely chiselled face faintly smiling above the designer summer-weight suit and blue silk shirt and tie he was wearing, and the tall, lean body relaxed. She could have kicked him. Hard. Very hard.

'I...I didn't know you were going to be here tonight?' As soon as she'd said it she realised it was a mistake. It suggested he was important enough to be mentioned in advance.

'Didn't I mention it?' Cassie entered the conversation now from her vantage point of interested spectator, and her voice was suspiciously offhand. 'I meant to give you a ring a couple of days ago, Robyn, but the twins are still playing up at night and with the way I am...' She laid a hand over her rounded stomach in a silent plea for sympathy. 'I'd forget my head if it wasn't screwed on,' she added with a winsome smile at Clay.

Believe that, believe anything. Their conversation of six days ago was suddenly crystal clear in Robyn's mind and she knew, she just *knew*, this was one of Cass's ruses. Her sister had decided that Clay would be the perfect business associate and had acted accordingly. Cass never let the grass grow under her feet.

'Jim got the opportunity to join Beryl at the conference—all expenses paid—so he rang us to explain, and it just so happened Clay was in town...' Cassie's voice dwindled away happily.

'How fortuitous,' Robyn said stolidly, her eyes holding her sister's until Cassie had the grace to look slightly discomfited. But only slightly. Still, Cass had no idea of the true state of affairs between she and Clay, Robyn reminded herself silently. Perhaps she should have told her a little of what had transpired all those years ago to avoid just such a situation as this one. *He was her partner for the evening.* As disasters went, it was a biggie.

'I'll leave Clay to look after you, then. I just need to go and check a couple of things in the kitchen.' Cassie managed to look faintly preoccupied as she drifted away although Robyn knew full well everything in the kitchen would be working like clockwork. Occasions like this were her sister's forte and always went like a dream due to painstaking preparation and careful planning.

'Let me get you a drink, Robyn. What would you like?'

If she told him what she would like—namely for him to be transported somewhere, *anywhere*, but here—it would be the death knell on poor Guy's birthday celebration. She could feel that her cheeks had cooled a little and she hoped her voice was several degrees below its normal warm tone when she said, 'A glass of white wine would be lovely, thank you.'

How had she allowed herself to be manoeuvred into such a truly horrific situation? As she watched Clay cross the room to the large circular marble table where all the drinks had been laid out for everyone to help themselves, Robyn's thoughts were racing. She was stupid. No, no not stupid, she corrected in the next moment. Too trusting. But then that implied that Cass meant her harm and she knew that was untrue. Whatever Cass had done she had done it with the very best of intentions.

Robyn's lips twitched ruefully. Cass was the epitome of the happily married housewife, blissfully content with Guy and the twins and over the moon at the prospect of a third child. The fact that Guy had the sort of job which meant his wife didn't have to work unless she wanted to suited her sister down to the ground. Cass was utterly domesticated; she even made her own bread on occasion and grew raspberries and strawberries, along with her own vegetables, in the garden, claiming she wanted her family to eat produce she knew was safe and wholesome. Their mother had often said Cass should have been born in the middle of the country—she'd have made a wonderful farmer's wife.

But... Robyn's eyes narrowed on Clay's tall frame as

he poured the wine. Her sister's habit of viewing the world through rose-coloured spectacles had distinct disadvantages to those around her at times, and never more so than now.

And then Clay straightened and turned and looked straight at her before she could blank her face, and she knew, when she saw the hard firm mouth twitch slightly, that he was well aware of her dislike and, worse, that it didn't bother him an iota.

'One glass of white wine.' His gravelly voice was very even and quiet as he handed her the drink on reaching her side, and Robyn forced hers into like mode as she answered, 'Thank you, Clay,' making sure her hand didn't inadvertently touch his.

'It is chilled.' The devastating eyes held hers with no effort. 'Although that's barely relevant in your case.'

'I'm sorry?' She raised her chin a fraction.

'You're frosty enough to take the wine down a good few degrees all by yourself,' he said pleasantly.

She stared at him, shocked by the suddenness and speed of the confrontation which—for one stunned moment—had robbed her of all coherent thought. And then she raised her small chin further in an angry movement which wasn't lost on the tall figure in front of her, and said, her voice crisp and steady, 'That's very rude, Mr Lincoln, considering we haven't met in years and I barely know you.'

'"Mr Lincoln" is going to go down like a lead balloon during the social repartee an occasion like this merits, and although we might not have met in years I'd say we know each other fairly well, all things considered,' he returned smoothly.

'Really?' Robyn could feel her face burning.

'Yes, really.' He smiled, his voice silky. 'I think you

were about twelve years' old when Guy first introduced me to your family, so I'd say the next three or four years count as a pretty good ''knowing'' period, wouldn't you?'

She was saved the effort of searching for an adequately scathing reply by one of the other couples who joined them at that precise moment, but as she made small talk and joined in the laughter and social niceties she was furious to find she couldn't ignore Clay as she wanted to.

The last years had evaporated as though they'd never been and she was like a sixteen-year-old schoolgirl again, conscious of his every movement, the low husky quality of his voice, the sheer physical appeal of him. The suit he was wearing couldn't even begin to disguise the unequivocally tough and hard male body inside it, and his closeness was playing havoc with her senses. Which was as ridiculous as it was humiliating.

There were at least eight other people in the room besides Clay and herself, but it was *his* warm male scent surrounding her, *his* voice that made her pulse race, *his* body that she was painfully and rawly aware of. She could feel the attraction so strongly she wouldn't have been surprised if the air had begun to crackle, but Clay seemed quietly relaxed and at ease as he chatted at her side to the other couple.

Mind you, there was no reason for him to be otherwise, she reminded herself tartly as she smiled and nodded at the woman opposite her who was regaling them with the latest achievement of the wonder child she had given birth to a few months previously.

She couldn't bring herself to believe he had forgotten the events of that awful evening twelve years ago—much as she would like to—but the whole thing obviously had meant absolutely nothing to him. If she had stayed in his memory at all, which she seriously doubted, it would have been as a ridiculous little girl who had overstepped the mark and in doing so had embarrassed them both. If he had been embarrassed, that was. Which she seriously doubted. Icebergs didn't embarrass as far as she knew.

'...at the moment, Robyn?'

'I'm sorry?' She came to with a jolt to realise May Jarvis, the wife of one of Guy's oldest friends, had asked her a question amid all the ramblings and she hadn't heard a word of it.

May's smile dimmed a little. 'I asked you if there was anyone special on the horizon at the moment?' she repeated.

Why was it that happily married matrons of her sister's age always seemed to assume they could ask any pertinent question they liked at dos like this one? Robyn asked herself tersely, before her innate sense of fair play made her feel guilty. May was only trying to include her in the conversation and make small talk, she reminded herself quickly, and normally she would have passed off such a question with a light, amusing comment. But tonight wasn't normal, and she was all out of light, amusing comments! She just wanted to go *home*.

'No.' She could feel the muscles at the back of her neck were as tight as piano wire and she had only been here ten minutes or so. How was she going to get through a whole evening?

'Oh.' May had clearly expected more and now she glanced across at her husband rather helplessly, who stared back at her with a face that seemed to say, What do you expect me to say?

It was Clay who spoke into the moment, his voice soothing and cool as he said quietly, 'I understand from Cassie that all Robyn's energies have been tied up in the business she's involved in. Is that right, Robyn?' he added smoothly.

Cass hadn't. She hadn't, had she? She wouldn't have mentioned the refusal of the business loan and everything surely? 'Yes, that's right,' she agreed evenly, gratified her voice was showing no sign of the turmoil within. She'd never forgive Cass!

'Oh, really? How interesting.' May was gushing but it was well-meant. 'What sort of business is it?'

'PR.' She couldn't just leave it at that, not after her abruptness before. 'I formed my own business a couple of years ago so it's pretty time-absorbing. If you want to get a foot on the ladder you have to put in all the hours it needs,' Robyn said quietly to May without looking Clay's way. 'There's plenty of competition who will be only too pleased to do it if you don't.'

'I can imagine.' May was genuinely sympathetic. 'I was involved in advertising before I had the baby and that's the same. Of course I didn't have my own company,' she added quickly, 'so I suppose the incentive wasn't quite the same. How many people do you employ?'

'Just one at the moment.' She would have given the world to massage the taut muscles at the nape of her neck but she didn't dare with those icy silver eyes watching her. 'But I'm hoping to expand in time of course.'

'So you're a career girl.' Clay had moved fractionally closer, his spicy aftershave subtly touching her oversensitised nerves, and Robyn willed herself to show no reaction at all. 'Funny, but I'd got you down as a hearth-and-home type back in the good old days,' he drawled with silky innocence.

'Oh, so you two go back a long way?' May was all ears.

'We don't go back at all,' Robyn said politely but

firmly, wondering how suave and debonair Clay would look with white wine dripping off the end of his nose. 'Clay was at university with Guy, that's all, and he used to come and see Cass and Guy in the holidays sometimes when I was just a kid.' It was dismissive.

She knew the dark, handsome face was surveying her with mockingly raised eyebrows and for that reason she didn't let her eyes connect with his. She wasn't the young, starry-eyed sixteen-year-old any more and she was darned if she would let him call the tune tonight. He had purposefully got May interested, she knew it, with his pointed reference to the good old days. The good old days! She gave a healthy snort in her mind. Good for whom? Not for her, that was sure.

Once Cassie had got them all seated at the table and the first course—baby spinach, avocado and crispy pancetta salad—had been served, it wasn't quite so bad.

Clay was sitting opposite her for one thing, and the few feet of space across the elaborate dining table which was a picture of glittering crystal and snowy-white linen and silver, was very welcome. May's husband was on one side of her and was quite attentive, and she knew Guy's friend, John, on her left, well, so she concentrated her conversation on them without being too obvious.

Nevertheless she noticed, with acid amusement, that Clay was charming the two women either side of him with no apparent effort on his part. They were twittering and giggling like teenagers! Still, from all she had heard over the last years he'd had plenty of practice at being a ladies' man since his young wife had died. Love 'em and leave 'em reputation, according to Guy. Which was fine, just fine if that was the way he wanted to live his life, Robyn thought nastily. A tom-cat always finds its own level.

Guy served a particularly delicious red wine with the

main course of pan-fried pork fillet with sage and spring onion mash, and the excellent food and good wine produced a calmingly mellow effect on her racing nerves. Especially when John refilled her glass twice. By the time Cassie brought out the triple-chocolate torte, along with an Eve's Pudding topped with caramelised sugar, Robyn was telling herself she was quite adult enough to handle this evening with dignity and aplomb. Clay Lincoln didn't bother her!

She'd got off on the wrong foot maybe, she admitted silently to herself, but nothing was lost, not really. The worst thing she could do, with an egoist like Clay Lincoln, was to let him think he affected her in any way. She would treat him just the same as she did everyone else: she'd be friendly, charming, amusing—everything one was at occasions like this. Once the meal was over a little polite chit-chat, a laugh or two, and then she would bow out gracefully as soon as the first couple made a move to leave and that would be that. Easy.

Cassie brought in Guy's pile of birthday presents from family and friends during the cheese and biscuits and, as Robyn left the table briefly to help Cassie in the kitchen with the coffee, her sister whispered, 'You'll never guess what Clay's given us for Guy's thirty-fifth. I still can't believe it. Once the baby's born and I'm feeling okay he's going to fly the five of us out to his beach house in Florida for a couple of weeks, all expenses paid. What do you think about that?'

'Really? That's wonderful, Cass.' Robyn was thrilled for them, really thrilled, but she couldn't help wishing it had been someone else who had provided the trip. Anyone else.

'Apparently you just step off the front porch straight onto white sand, but there's an indoor pool as well and the use of one of Clay's cars for the fortnight, and a housekeeper who will do all the cooking. It's just too good to be true,' Cassie beamed happily. 'It really is.'

Bit like Clay Lincoln, then.

For an awful moment Robyn thought she had said the words out loud but when Cassie's sunny face didn't change, she knew the sarcasm had been in her mind only. 'How often have you and Guy seen Clay over the last years?' she asked carefully as she tipped the box of peppermint creams onto a silver plate and placed them on the serving trolley. 'Isn't a present like this a bit...extreme?' she suggested expressionlessly.

'According to Guy, Clay's like that, unpredictable. And Guy's seen him now and again; they go out to lunch mostly although Clay has been to dinner once or twice. He's got a mansion-type place in Windsor apparently although we've never been there. He is always jet-setting here, there and everywhere—he's never in one place for more than a few days, Guy says. Course, with all his business interests, you'd expect that.'

Robyn nodded. 'What does he do exactly?' she asked quietly as Cassie loaded the trolley with another plate of dark chocolates, slices of shortbread and jugs of steaming coffee, sugar, milk and whipped cream. Her sister always made sure everyone ate to excess.

'Well, I understand his father was in shipping,' Cassie said in a low voice, 'but Clay's diversified into property and one or two other things as well. Fingers in plenty of pies.'

'A real entrepreneur,' Robyn said lightly, keeping all trace of expression out of her voice with some effort. Filthy rich and with an ego to match. Just what she had thought in fact. She had been blind to everything but his overwhelming attraction and dark charisma at sixteen; it was different now. *She* was different.

When she and Cassie re-entered the room Robyn was aware of Clay's eyes on her but she didn't look his way, keeping her gaze on Guy at the head of the table. 'Coffee for the birthday boy?' she called brightly. 'Black or white, Guy?'

'Black, by the look of him,' Cassie commented a trifle wryly at her side as she glanced at her husband's flushed face and vacant grin. 'I don't fancy having to carry him up the stairs.'

Everyone lingered over coffee and brandy, the atmosphere mellow and comfortable as witticisms flashed back and forth and laughter reverberated in increasing waves of hilarity. Cassie was sitting basking in the glow of a supremely successful dinner party and Guy was surveying his guests with the air of a man who was truly satisfied with life. Robyn envied them. They had found each other as well as their niche in life and that was a double blessing. And then, as her gaze left Guy's smiling, flushed, contented face it was drawn to the ice-blue eyes across the table and she found her breath catch in her throat at the mocking, mordacious quality to Clay's hooded regard.

He was surveying them all in much the same way as a dispassionate scientist with a load of bugs under a microscope, she reflected angrily. How dared he? How *dared* he consider himself so far above the rest of them? Who did he think he was anyway?

'I think Guy's enjoyed his thirty-fifth, don't you?' The low drawl was just for her ears and although Robyn longed to tell him not to be so darn supercilious she knew she couldn't. It was unthinkable to put a spanner in the works of Cassie and Guy's evening. So instead she was forced to grit her teeth and give him a frosty little smile.

His eyes narrowed briefly but in the next moment she broke the hold and turned to John, and she made sure she didn't glance Clay's way again as she finished her coffee.

How was it, she asked herself silently, that all her previous good intentions of being distantly charming and amusing could be shattered with one glance from the man? In all the last twelve years she hadn't met anyone who could set her teeth on edge like Clay Lincoln. Everything, but *everything* about him grated on her. She couldn't imagine why he and Guy were friends.

She wasn't going to wait for someone else to make the first move to leave. As soon as it was decently possible she would make her goodbyes and be out of here; she didn't need this. She really, *really* didn't need this. She would rather die than let Clay see it but she was acutely aware of every little movement he made and it was mortifying. Suddenly she just didn't know herself any more and she was aghast at the way she felt.

Music was drifting in from the lounge, courtesy of Frank Sinatra who was doing it 'his way', and as Cassie began ushering them all out of their seats Robyn seized the opportunity to take her sister's arm and say quietly, 'I really need to be making tracks, Cass, I'm sorry. It's been a lovely evening but—'

'You can't go yet.' Cassie was horrified. 'It's only half past ten for goodness' sake! Here, grab one of the bottles of brandy and port and bring them through, would you?' And with that she sailed off across the hall, where she could be heard urging everyone to replenish their glasses.

Robyn stared after her, biting her lower lip and wondering how she could love someone and want to strangle them at the same time. It was a feeling she'd had before but never so strongly.

She had just turned to reach for the bottles when she

saw Clay, still seated, surveying her with contemplative eyes. 'Somewhere else to go?' he asked mildly.

At some point in the evening he had discarded his suit jacket over the back of his chair and had undone the first couple of buttons of his shirt, pulling his tie loose, and although she was absolutely furious with herself the sheer physical magnetism of him registered in her solar plexus like a fist. She could feel the blood pulsing through her veins, a frantic flood that made her feel breathless and giddy, and she had to swallow hard before she could say, 'Not—not exactly. Only home. But I've a heap of work waiting for me.'

'At half past ten at night?' he queried softly.

She flushed hotly, her voice something of a snap as she said, 'I meant tomorrow, of course. It will mean an early start and so I didn't want to be too late tonight.' He needn't try and be clever!

'Do you always work such long hours?' He stood up as he spoke, his silver eyes running over her face and the cloud of silky red-gold curls falling to below her slender shoulders. 'I thought everyone was due one day of rest a week.'

She shrugged carefully. At five feet nine she had never considered herself petite but Clay must be at least another six inches taller and it was disconcerting to find she was having to look up at him. 'It varies,' she said stiffly.

'Are you always so communicative?' he drawled silkily.

They were the only two people left in the dining room now and Robyn had the ridiculous urge to turn and bolt into the lounge, but the knowledge that he would love that, just *love* it, restrained her. 'I don't know what you mean,' she said tightly, reaching for the bottle of brandy and another of port as she added, 'Cass wants these, I'd better take them through.'

'Running away...again?' The pause was just long enough to bring the colour which had begun to recede from her cheeks surging back with renewed vigour.

'I beg your pardon?' she said with icy dignity, her voice at direct variance with her fiery skin. Horrible, *horrible* man!

'If you had known I would be here tonight you wouldn't have come.' It was a statement, not a question.

You've never said a truer word, she thought. 'Don't flatter yourself,' she returned scathingly. 'How could your whereabouts be of any possible interest to me one way or the other?'

He hadn't liked that. Robyn was immensely gratified to see his mouth tighten, but the black scowl was a little unnerving and grasping the bottles she made for the door. Enough was enough.

'You're an angel.' As she entered the lounge where the others were draped about talking and laughing, a couple of the women dancing languidly to the music, Cassie took the bottles from her, glancing interestedly over her shoulder. 'Where's Clay?'

'How would I know?' Robyn said offhandedly. 'Bathroom perhaps?' Her tone made it quite clear she couldn't care less.

'Robyn, make an effort *please*,' Cassie hissed quietly. 'That's not too much to ask, is it? He's—'

What he was Robyn never found out as the next moment Clay walked in the room and Cassie fluttered over to him, insisting on replenishing his glass and then—to Robyn's horror—drawing him over to Robyn as she said loudly, 'You know you two have *so* much in common when you think about it, both with your own businesses and so on. You're both workaholics, you know,' and she giggled in a most un-Cassie-like way.

'Clay and I have nothing in common, Cass.' It was out before she could stop it, his narrowed eyes and cold face hitting a multitude of nerves, and she hastily qualified the retort with, 'Clay is a millionaire with a network of businesses that stretch from here to Timbuktu, and I'm a one-man-band in Kensington. You really can't compare the two.'

'Timbuktu is a town in central Mali on the River Niger, and to my knowledge I have no business connections there,' Clay said pleasantly, his voice conversational and his eyes deadly, 'and I am sure your company is every bit as important to you as mine are to me. I think that is what your sister was getting at.'

She knew what Cassie was getting at but she couldn't very well say so, Robyn thought helplessly, knowing she had been put in her place by an expert. She glared at him, hating him for making her feel such an ungracious, churlish boor, and then as Cassie shifted uncomfortably at the side of them Robyn tried to straighten her face into a more acceptable expression.

'Robyn works too hard, Clay.' Cassie was clearly in 'in for a penny, in for a pound' mode. 'I know she's trying to build the business up but nothing is worth killing yourself for. Of course it doesn't help that her bank manager is less than far-sighted,' she finished with all the delicacy of a charging bull-elephant.

Dinner party or no dinner party, this was finale time. 'Excuse me.' Robyn's voice was throbbing with outrage as she nodded at Clay, taking Cassie's arm in a vise-like grip as she did so and hauling her sister out of the room before anyone could say another word.

She didn't let go until the pair of them were safely in

the kitchen with the door shut behind them, and then she pushed her sister onto one of the breakfast stools with the command of, '*Sit*,' her face flushed and her brown eyes sparking.

'Robyn, please, just let me explain—'

'Not another word, Cass.' She was angry, so angry her voice choked before she took a deep breath and continued. 'You've gone too far and you know it, don't you? If I had wanted my private business broadcast to all and sundry I would have said so. Everything I tell you is in confidence, and you knew—you *knew*—Clay was the last person I'd want to confide in. I couldn't have made it plainer the other day,' she finished vehemently.

'I'm sorry.' Cassie didn't look at her and her voice was meek.

'Sorry isn't enough, Cass. You tricked me into coming tonight too. You didn't even give me the chance of refusing when you knew Guy's brother wasn't going to make it. Well, I'm going now and I tell you it'll be a long time before I forgive you for this. I mean it!' Robyn's voice was high with outrage.

Cassie had always been unsquashable and pregnancy had only served to make her more serene. She raised her eyes now, her voice placid and her face composed as she said, 'He would be perfect for what you need, Robyn. His own businesses are so vast he wouldn't meddle or get involved with yours, but with just a fraction of what he's worth backing you you'd never look back. And he's a friend of the family. It's *ideal*.'

'He's a friend of yours and Guys, Cass, let's get that straight. I don't know him; I don't want to know him and if I ever see him again in all my life it'll be too soon!'

They both heard the knock on the kitchen door and spun round to face it, and it dawned on Robyn—Cassie too, by the look on her face—that the person outside must have heard every word of that last statement because Robyn's voice had not been moderate.

Robyn knew who it would be before the door opened and Clay's dark cool voice spoke. It went with the whole miserable evening somehow. She prepared herself for the explosion.

'Do I take it this is a bad moment?' He was speaking directly to Cassie; Robyn might not have existed. 'Guy asked me to tell you that May and her husband are leaving; babysitter deadlines.'

'Oh, yes, yes, of course. I must... Yes.' If Clay hadn't had a grain of intelligence Cassie's flustered voice and scarlet face would have alerted him to the fact that he just might have heard something personally detrimental.

But Clay *was* intelligent, formidably so, Robyn thought miserably as she watched her sister skuttle out of the room as though the devil himself was at her heels. But the devil wasn't following Cass, he was here with her, she acknowledged silently, as icy eyes drilled into her. 'So...' It was grim. 'I see the spoilt brat is still a spoilt brat?'

'What?' She couldn't believe her ears. 'What did you say?'

'I should imagine you will rise to the top of the tree with very little effort,' the devastatingly cold voice continued gratingly. 'Ignoring anything you don't want to acknowledge, bulldozing your way through without a thought of anyone else or any higher concepts—the business world will just love you, Robyn. Do you use that delectable body as well as your brain to get what you want? You started early, I should know that, so—'

Nothing in the world could have stopped her lashing out at him and it caught him completely off guard. His head snapped back with the force of her hand across his face and for a moment there was complete stillness in the kitchen, the sound of voices and music from outside unbearably normal in what was suddenly a terribly abnormal world.

Robyn was shaking now, her dark brown eyes enormous in her chalk-white face. She could see her hand print forming on one tanned cheek, the red lines a reproach in themselves, and she stared at him, shocked beyond measure at what she had done. She had never, in all her life, struck anyone, and for it to be Clay Lincoln! And at Guy's birthday party!

And then she backed away as Clay came forwards without saying a word, his face frightening. 'Don't...don't you dare hit me. I'll call for someone—'

'Hit you?' It stopped him in his tracks. He swore, softly but vehemently and with enough force to scare her further. 'Is that the sort of man you think I am? The sort who strikes women?'

'I don't know what sort of man you are.'

'Really?' It was deadly. 'And yet you've been insufferable all evening. Care to tell me why?' he asked cuttingly.

She had backed as far as she could go, the edge of the sink pressing into her lower back, but she still drew herself up as she said, 'Me, insufferable? *Me?*'

'Oh, don't tell me!' He folded muscled arms over his broad chest. 'I'm the one who's been aching to pick a fight. Right?'

'I—I haven't wanted to pick a fight, merely...' Her voice trailed away. How could you explain the unexplainable?

'Yes?' He was eyeing her with complete and utter disdain.

She set her jaw, the old defiance which had been severely shaken coming to her aid. 'I don't have to explain anything to you,' she stated tightly. 'Not a thing!'

'Wrong.' He was watching her with unrelenting eyes, and then something in his expression changed as he added, thoughtfully now, 'You don't add up, Miss Brett, and I don't like that. I remember a somewhat precocious teenager, bright, undeniably lovely, but fresh, eager, alive. There wasn't a trace of sourness or scepticism there, so what happened?'

You. You happened. You blew my word apart and you don't have the faintest inkling, do you? From his comment labelling her precocious and a spoilt brat as a teenager, he'd obviously put his own interpretation on that night years ago. He'd imagined she'd been trying out her new-found womanhood on any available man, was that it? That he had been the luck of the draw on which to cut her puppy teeth? Whereas in reality...

And that crack about using her body to get what she wanted! He had made it quite plain how he viewed her now as well. He was hateful, *loathsome*. How ever could she have imagined herself in love with him? She must have been stark staring mad!

'Cass will be concerned if I don't get back to the others,' she said stiffly, 'so if you've quite finished?'

'I haven't even started,' he said softly, but he stood aside for her to pass him, his dark face unfathomable.

If she had been thinking straight she might have known he wouldn't just let her leave, not after all that had transpired, but her head was a whirl and hot emotion sat in the place where common sense normally dwelt.

She swept past him, only to find herself swung round by hard male fingers on her wrist and then she was in his arms before she realised what was happening.

'Let go of—' The rest of her words were smothered by

his mouth on hers and for a heart-stopping second she was too surprised and bewildered to react. And then she struggled fiercely, fighting him with all her strength. It had about as much impact as a moth fluttering against a brick wall.

It was a challenging kiss, severe almost, a kiss that dared her to relax and enjoy it, and it was a kiss by an expert. That much registered on Robyn's spinning senses. He felt hard and sure against her softness and the smell of him spun intoxicatingly in her head, bringing her skin alive from the tips of her toes to the crown of her head.

His name was whispering deep inside her and that frightened her as much as the sensations he was drawing forth so effortlessly. Clay was the last person in the world she should want to make love to her and shockingly—humiliatingly—that was exactly what she did want. Which made her…what? The answer to that gave her the strength to jerk away with a suddenness that took him by surprise.

'I hate you.' It was raw and low and she was trembling.

'Do you?' He looked back at her, his silver eyes glittering slightly. 'Why such a strong emotion, Robyn?' he asked tauntingly.

She blinked a little. He was tying her up in knots and she was letting him; this was completely the wrong way to handle a man like Clay Lincoln. She knew that; she dealt with all types in her work including hard-bitten journalists who would sell their own mother for a story, so why had her normal cool, distant façade got blown to smithereens? What was it about this man?

'I don't appreciate being mauled about for a start,' she bit out tightly, praying the trembling in the pit of her stomach wouldn't communicate itself through her voice.

'Mauled?' He gave a soft, mocking laugh as he stepped

back a pace, the crystal eyes pinning her to the spot. 'I don't think so, Robyn.'

His impossibly light eyes reflected his contempt of the statement and his aggressive handsomeness, his utter surety in himself, was galling. For a moment Robyn had the insane impulse to throw a paddy and shout and scream, *anything*, to get under that tanned skin, but the knowledge that she would be acting like the spoilt brat he'd accused her of being was restraint enough.

'You may not think so but that is what I call it when a man forces himself on a woman,' she said icily. 'I neither asked for or wanted you to kiss me.'

'True.' And he had the absolute affront to smile. 'But you enjoyed it when I did. I've kissed enough women in my time to know that. I had wondered all night what you'd taste like and now I know.'

She didn't believe this man! She glared at him, bristling with fury, her fingers itching to hit him again. What an incredibly colossal ego. But she was not going to give him the satisfaction of losing her temper again. She drew herself up to her full five feet nine inches and stared straight into the silver-blue orbs, her voice dripping with scorn as she said, 'You need to think I enjoyed it; that's quite a different thing. If it makes you happy, dream on, Mr Lincoln.'

Her tone of voice did not amuse him, that much was obvious, but before he could respond the door to the kitchen opened again and Cassie breezed in, her voice bright as she said, 'You two still in here? I told you you'd have plenty in common, didn't I? You wouldn't carry the ice bucket through for me, would you, Clay?' she added as she opened the freezer door and extracted a bag of ice cubes to refill the huge silver ice bucket she had brought in with her from the lounge.

'Sure thing.' It was cool and relaxed, insultingly so.

Sure thing. Robyn stood for a moment more after the other two had walked through to the lounge. And did he think she was a sure thing too? Like all the women who flocked to his dark aura? Thought he only had to click his fingers, no doubt.

Think again, Clay Lincoln. She drew her lips together, her brown eyes narrowing. This was one man she wouldn't touch with a barge pole. And she was out of here, *right now*.

CHAPTER THREE

'So how was the dinner party last night? Cassie serve up salmonella along with the main course, or is there another reason why you look like you ought to be in bed this morning?' Drew's voice was light but her baby-blue eyes were anxious as she surveyed Robin's white face.

'I'm fine, Drew.' Robyn had just opened the door to her assistant and now she stood aside, waving Drew in as she said, 'The coffee pot's on.'

'Robyn, you look awful.' Never one to beat about the bush Drew turned to face her after Robyn had shut the door. 'Go back to bed, I can manage here.'

That was ridiculous and they both knew it. They had a product launch for a cosmetic company the next day and Robyn had fought off some powerful competition to acquire it. Everything had to be faultless and flawless; she had promised a polished launch with maximum flair and that meant working until late evening as it was, and then a six o'clock start on Monday morning.

'I'm all right, really.' Robyn managed a fairly normal smile in spite of the fact she hadn't slept a wink all night and had been downstairs at her desk by five. 'I just didn't sleep well, that's all,' she added with a fair attempt at nonchalance.

'Have you eaten breakfast?' And at Robyn's shake of the head Drew scolded, 'And I bet you were up at the crack of dawn too! Honestly, Robyn, sometimes I think you haven't got the sense you were born with. You can't work like you do and skip meals. I'll make some toast and you'll sit and eat it before you do anything else.'

'Thanks, Mum.' But Robyn was laughing now. This was the other side of Drew that few people saw—the fussy, motherly side—and it was a complete antithesis to the dizzy, frivolous image the attractive blonde normally projected. But then, who knew what anyone else was really like? Robyn thought soberly as Drew bustled off upstairs. Certainly Clay didn't have the faintest idea what or who she was.

And then she caught herself angrily. No more thinking about Clay Lincoln! She'd wasted all the night hours fretting and walking the floor, and who cared what he thought about her anyway. He'd labelled her an empty-headed, amorous little flirt at sixteen who'd been ready and willing to jump into bed with any male, and now she'd risen to a sour, ruthless-minded business woman who wasn't averse to using her body to get what she wanted.

She ground her teeth, furious with herself because it still rankled. Because it shouldn't matter. He was nothing. *Nothing.*

She had left Cass's immediately after the episode in the kitchen, pleading a headache, and she hadn't looked at Clay once, not even when she had said goodbye. Even then she had kept her gaze somewhere behind his left ear.

But somehow—and this was the worst thing of all—she couldn't get the memory of what that kiss had done to her out of her head and her senses. She touched her lips unconsciously, her eyes wide and unseeing. How could she have responded like that to a man she loathed and detested? He was dangerous. He was so, so dangerous. And unprincipled. And base. And—

She was saved from further reflection by Drew calling

down to say she was fixing scrambled eggs on toast and Robyn must come *now*, not a minute, not a second later.

The two women worked non-stop for the rest of the day with just a ten-minute break at lunch for sandwiches and more coffee, and after Robyn had waved Drew off at just gone five o'clock she continued at her desk until her brain was as scrambled as the eggs at breakfast and the sky was pitch black outside.

After a long hot bath which she had to vacate when she found herself sliding under the water, having fallen fast asleep, Robyn took a mug of hot chocolate and a plate of her favourite shortbread biscuits to bed with her, snuggling down under the duvet as soon as she'd finished after setting her alarm clock for five the next morning. The early start was essential with all she had to do.

She was asleep as soon as her head touched the pillow and woke just before the alarm the next morning, her mind focused on the launch, and the hard work of the day before paying dividends with the facts and figures she had at her fingertips.

The day went well and everything ran like clockwork, which was fortuitous as due to a last minute problem with another client Drew had had to stay in Kensington and didn't accompany Robyn to the launch as they'd planned. But it wasn't ideal; the same thing could happen again when Drew *would* be needed, Robyn thought to herself as she drove home that evening. She'd had several approaches by prospective clients that very day, and very soon it was going to be case of refusing work she wanted to take which would break her heart, or gambling on the quality of service she could give which wasn't an option. She was caught between the devil and the deep blue sea.

She was still mulling over the conundrum when she

arrived back in Kensington and parked the car outside her house, which was probably why she didn't notice the low-slung Aston Martin sports car several yards away...

'Hi, Robyn.' A very flustered, pink-cheeked Drew sprang up from her desk as Robyn stepped into the office, but Robyn wasn't looking at her assistant. Her horrified eyes were fixed on the large, lean figure sprawled in one of the easy chairs at the side of the room, a cup of coffee in his hands and an innocent—too innocent—expression on his face.

'What are you doing here?' she snapped abruptly.

It was ungracious to put it mildly, but Clay's voice was the epitome of charm as he drawled, 'Hello, Robyn. Drew's been looking after me admirably, as you can see.'

She didn't care if Drew had been looking after him or not! Or rather she wished Drew hadn't let him over the threshold let alone fed him coffee. 'I asked you what you're doing here,' she repeated tightly, her face straight and her eyes narrowing on his cool, relaxed countenance. He had a nerve!

He looked marvellous. That thought was as unwelcome as the realisation that her heart was doing its level best to jump out of her chest. He had been smooth and suave and sophisticated Saturday night, and he was still all those things, but the black silk shirt open at the neck and dark charcoal trousers he was wearing today took the brooding maleness inherent in his attractiveness to another dimension.

'I called by to see you of course.' The husky voice was as deep and disturbing as ever, and Robyn had to force herself not to betray the shiver of awareness it produced in the core of her being, but it was unnerving. *He* was unnerving.

'Why?' she asked stiffly, fighting hard to keep cool.

'To renew our old friendship?' he suggested silkily.

Robyn just stared at him, her mind racing as she prayed with silent desperation that Cassie hadn't revealed anything of her business predicament after her warnings to her sister Saturday night. Please, God, not that. She couldn't bear that.

Her prayer was in vain.

'And to perhaps suggest a new one,' Clay continued smoothly.

'A new one?' Robyn was aware of Drew shifting uncomfortably at the side of them. 'We were never friends, Clay,' she said tightly.

'No?' The devastating ice-blue eyes surveyed the tall slender woman in front of him, the silver gaze taking in Robyn's warm creamy skin, wide, heavily lashed velvet eyes and mass of rich red-gold curls. 'Perhaps we weren't at that,' he drawled slowly.

'Then, I repeat, why are you here?'

'I would like to be your sleeping partner, Robyn,' Clay said with magnificent coolness.

Robyn heard Drew's swift intake of breath at the side of her. The other woman had obviously been wondering if she'd done the wrong thing in letting this six-foot-plus dreamboat in the front door by the warmth of Robyn's reception of him, and now she clearly couldn't believe her ears.

Robyn hated to spoil what was undoubtedly the highlight of Drew's otherwise unremarkable day, but... 'You've been talking to Cass,' she said flatly, before turning to Drew and adding, 'Business, Drew. We're just talking business here, so don't go running away with any fancy ideas, okay?'

'I wouldn't dream...I mean, it's nothing to do with me, and you're not the sort— That is...'

Robyn took pity on Drew's ramblings and touched the other woman's arm as she said, her voice soothing, 'Mr Lincoln is a friend of Cass's and my sister decided I needed a partner in the business when the bank manager was unforthcoming recently. That's all.' Drew knew all about the dilemma Robyn was in.

'Right.' Drew nodded, her pretty face expressing something that looked suspiciously like disappointment. Like Cass, she was forever encouraging Robyn to find herself a man, and as men went this one was sheer dynamite.

'Look, Drew, why don't you nip off now,' Robyn added quietly. 'You've put in a long day and you were here all day yesterday; I don't want to work you to death.'

'Are you sure?' Drew's gaze flashed to Clay's dark face for a moment and then back to Robyn's. In spite of this hunk being the sort of guy only found in dreams, Robyn didn't seem too happy he was here. 'I'm not in any rush.'

'Quite sure.' Robyn understood what Drew was not saying and appreciated the concern, but what she had to say to Clay Lincoln was best said without an audience, especially one that couldn't keep her eyes off him!

She had to keep control of this situation; it was already escalating into something acutely embarrassing, thanks to her sister. She needed to be firm and polite when she made it clear she had no intention of taking advantage of his offer, which had clearly been made as a favour to Cass and Guy. She didn't doubt Clay could afford to buy and sell a thousand little concerns like hers ten times over, but he was an astute businessman first and foremost and would never normally entertain such an undertaking. She was small fry, as much beneath his notice as an ant scurrying about on the ground and the last thing she needed— *the very last*—was any favours from Clay Lincoln.

As the door closed behind Drew, Clay settled further

in the chair, much to Robyn's silent irritation, and drawled softly, 'So, the help's gone; we're alone and now you can couch your refusal in the manner you prefer.'

He was watching her intently in spite of the apparent easy nonchalance, perhaps waiting for a visible reaction to the provocative statement, but Robyn was determined not to give him the satisfaction of showing any emotion. She walked across to her desk which was at the far end of the room next to the large window which looked out onto the small paved garden surrounded by flowering shrubs—she'd decided on a garden which embodied no maintenance at all—and perched on the edge of it before she said, calmly and with little expression, 'It is very kind of you, of course, but Cass had no right to mention the matter to you. I am not looking for a partner, Mr Lincoln.'

'Yes, you are, but not this particular one.'

It was said in such an easy conversational tone that for a moment the portent of his words didn't register. And then, as the confrontational nature of his statement dawned on Robyn her cheeks burnt with the quick resentment only Clay seemed able to ignite and her small jaw clenched in anger. Okay, if he wanted to do this the hard way that was fine by her, she thought hotly. 'If that's what you think, why bother to come in the first place?' she asked coldly.

'Good question.' He rose as he spoke, stretching like a long, lean cat and strolling down the room to lean against the wall opposite her desk, the strange silver-blue eyes never leaving her flushed face for a moment. She waited, but he didn't speak.

'Well?' She was determined not to be intimidated. She hadn't asked him to come here; she didn't owe him a thing.

The carved lips twitched a little and she could have

sworn he found the situation amusing. That, more than anything else, put iron in her backbone. She would *not* be laughed at.

'Perhaps I wanted to?' he suggested with a softness that carried an edge of steel now.

'Or perhaps you felt you had to?' she returned bitterly. 'I know my sister when she gets the bit between her teeth, Mr Lincoln: she doesn't give up. At the moment Cass's mission in life is to see me successful and happy, and she thinks the only way that can be achieved is for this business to take off with a bang. She's wrong.'

'She's a good person; you two are very fortunate to have such a warm relationship.'

Robyn was taken aback. There had been something in his voice she couldn't place but it had wiped away the hidden amusement she'd sensed a few moments ago. 'Yes, she is a good person,' she said after a pause. 'She's my best friend as well as my sister. I can't remember a time when Cass wasn't there for me.'

He nodded slowly, his eyes like polished crystal which threw the ebony blackness of his hair into more startlingly sharp relief. Those eyes had been with her in her dreams for years, she realised suddenly. She'd never seen anyone else with such amazingly beautiful cold eyes. 'Like I said, you're very fortunate,' he reiterated softly. 'Both of you.'

She stared at him as steadily as she could and hoped it disguised the fact that she was feeling totally out of her depth. Something had shifted in the last few seconds and she couldn't put her finger on it, but whatever it was, it was very real.

'Have you had dinner?' he asked with a marked lack of expression.

'What?' And then she collected herself and managed to say quickly, 'No, I've been at a launch all day and left as soon as I could to relieve Drew. I'll have something later. I'm...I'm very tired,' she added pointedly.

'All the more reason to let me buy you dinner,' he returned smartly. 'I'm sure you don't feel like fixing something yourself.'

Dinner? Was he quite insane? They hadn't said a civil word to each other since they'd met again after all these years and he wanted to buy her dinner? This was taking loyalty and friendship to Cassie and Guy too far!

'And, before you say anything, it is because I want to, not because I feel obliged because of your sister or anything else,' Clay said smoothly, reading her mind with an ease that alarmed her. 'I leave for the States first thing in the morning and I'll be away some time so it's a one-off, don't panic.'

It was the mockery that did it. He was acting as though he thought she was frightened to have dinner with him, and nothing could have fired Robyn's quick temper more effectively. She stiffened, her chin rising unconsciously and her beautiful brown eyes turning dark as she said, her voice clipped and short, 'Thank you, Mr Lincoln, dinner would be very nice.'

'Just one thing...' he was smiling again, a sort of cat-with-the-cream smile that made her think she might just have played straight into his hands. '...cut the "Mr Lincoln" would you? It's beginning to make me feel like a nineteenth-century headmaster, and Clay isn't too difficult to get the tongue round.' He raised dark eyebrows mockingly.

She'd just agreed to have dinner with him! Robyn's mind was racing. And she'd thought him the insane one! Whatever had made her rise to his particular brand of provocation like that? And why was he bothering with her anyway? He'd done his duty to Cass and Guy: he'd offered his help and she had refused him and that should have been that. She'd have thought he would have been breathing a silent sigh of relief at having got off so lightly. Oh, hell, none of this made sense. *She* didn't make sense. She should never have agreed to go out with him tonight.

'I'll have to change first.' She gestured at her clothes which had become somewhat crumpled throughout the day and were very definitely smartly functional rather than evening wear. 'Would you like to wait upstairs?' she added after a reluctant pause, hoping against hope he would refuse the invitation.

She couldn't have explained why but she didn't want him to impinge into her living quarters. The office was different: this was practical space and as utilitarian as any other office, but her home was *her*. There were a lot of dreams woven into the next two floors and every cushion, every ornament or picture, had been chosen by her because she loved it. She had waited months sometimes before she could afford something or other—like the red voile drapes at the window. She had spotted them in a wickedly expensive shop, the borders being hand-sewn with exquisite tiny lacy leaves, but she had known nothing else would do and had tacked a couple of sheets at the window until she could afford the drapes. And it had been worth it. But now Clay Lincoln's cynical, razor-sharp gaze was going to be able to dissect her inner self—or that's what it felt like.

But she was being silly. Robyn spoke sternly to herself as she walked across the office towards the stairs, Clay following behind her. For some reason this man still affected her in a way none other did, but she could get a handle on this. She *had* to get a handle on this!

'The bathroom and kitchen are on this floor.' Robyn gestured towards the rooms as they passed but didn't stop climbing the stairs until they reached the large through-room at the top of the house, and then she stood aside for Clay to precede her.

She was glad a mild golden sunlight was slanting through the windows at the end of the room and showing the colour scheme to its best advantage, along with high-lighting the pretty tubs of flowers she had bought for the tiny balcony a couple of weekends before.

The vibrant splashes of colour outside the windows drew the eyes and made the space in between appear even larger, encouraging the onlooker to look out into the wide expanse of blue sky beyond.

'What a lovely room.' Clay's voice was genuinely appreciative, but Robyn couldn't see his face as his back was towards her as he walked towards the balcony. 'In fact this whole house is lovely, unusual. Did you have an interior designer or was it like this when you bought it?'

'No and no.' He turned as she spoke, and she had to remind herself to show no outward reaction as every defence mechanism in her body came alive in response to his overwhelming maleness. 'The office was a small sitting room and separate kitchen, the bathroom was where it is but with a bedroom next door, and this floor consisted of two bedrooms. I had builders in for what seemed like the whole of my life but eventually they left and I could get on with decorating.'

'And you designed it all? Planned it?'

He sounded amazed and she was annoyed with herself at how pleased she felt. It didn't *matter* if he approved of her or not—at least it shouldn't. She nodded, adding, 'I enjoyed it, it was fun. My grandmother left me some money—Cass and I both—and I used mine for this place. My own home, and the business too of course. I always had that in the back of my mind and it seemed like the right time, a once-in-a-lifetime chance.'

'A lady who knows her own mind and what she wants in life.'

It was said quietly and evenly, almost without expression, but as Robyn looked into the eyes which resembled silver ice under a blue winter sky she felt there was criticism under the surface. And as always she met the challenge head-on. 'You disapprove of that?' she asked directly. 'Going for what you want?'

'Should I?' he returned with coolly lifted eyebrows.

It was no answer but hot and sticky as she was, after a hectic day when she hadn't even had time to renew her make-up or check her hair, Robyn was in no state to press the matter. For the time being at least. But she hadn't liked that little remark.

Clay looked as cool and well-groomed as if he had recently stepped out of the shower into fresh clothes—which he might well have done for all she knew. Robyn conceded temporary defeat and smiled brightly. 'Help yourself to a drink, the cocktail cabinet is cunningly disguised in that little cupboard,' she said lightly, pointing to the bottom of the pine dresser which sat with the table and chairs. 'I won't be long.'

'Take all the time you need.' And then he smiled.

Robyn stood transfixed, hypnotised. She'd forgotten that smile. How could she have forgotten that smile? It had always had the power to transform the devastatingly hard handsomeness into something much more lethal, softening the chiselled features as it did and bringing a warm silkiness to the piercing eyes.

He had smiled at her like that the first time Guy had brought him to the house to meet Cass; it had been that very moment, at the age of twelve, she had fallen hope-lessly in love with him...

But that was the past. She dragged in a secret breath and schooled her face into a careful smile, turning away as she said, 'Turn the TV on if you like.'

She almost went headlong down the stairs, and it was at that point she warned herself not to dredge up any more memories from the past. Clay Lincoln in the present was more than enough to cope with and she needed all her wits about her.

She ran a shallow bath and stripped off her clothes quickly. She was out of the water again in a couple of minutes, padding out onto the landing in her long towelling robe and then standing in front of the long fitted cupboard that served as her wardrobe for valuable minutes as she mentally discarded one outfit after another, working herself into a real tizzy in the process.

'Oh, get a grip, girl.' She shut her eyes tightly as she breathed out the admonition but her head was whirling. Somehow Clay was back in her life and it terrified her.

No, no it didn't. Her eyes snapped open and the inner voice was savage. He was *nothing* to her so how could he have any effect on her, she told herself fiercely. She would have dinner with him because there was nothing else she could do in the circumstances, but once tonight was over then that would be that. By his own admission he was planing to be away some time and in the inter-vening period she would make it crystal clear to Cass exactly why she never wanted to see Clay Lincoln again. It would be both painful and humiliating to reveal the past and her part in what had been a disastrous episode, but she should have told her sister years ago. She saw that now.

Robyn reached inside the wardrobe and took the first

dress she came to off the hanger. She wasn't going to worry about how she looked either. No titivating.

The dress was a plain one in dark brown wool and she'd never particularly liked it. She stared at it for a moment in her hands, bit her lip at her own inconsistency, and then replaced it quickly before selecting an olive-green cashmere dress that was gathered at the neck and fell to just below her knees. It had cost her an arm and a leg at the beginning of the winter a few months ago, but it fitted like a dream and turned her size twelve into a size eight by some magic all of its own. She'd managed to find some strappy shoes of exactly the same colour and now she pulled those out, dressing quickly and frowning at herself when her hands shook as she fixed big gold hoops in her ears in the bathroom.

What was the matter with her for goodness' sake? She was twenty-eight years old. A competent business woman in charge of her own life and career. She was not—repeat *not*, she emphasised firmly—a starry-eyed, naïve school-girl any more.

She looked at her reflection in the mirror and wide dark eyes stared back at her. Hair up or down? More sophisticated up, more sexy down. It went up, with a few curling tendrils to soften the style, and after applying a touch of green eyeshadow to her eyelids and thickening her already thick lashes a little more with black mascara she was nearly ready. Deep red lipstick completed her hasty toilet, a long deep breath steadied her racing nerves and, after dabbing a little of the Givenchy perfume one of her friends had bought her for Christmas on her wrists, she shut the bathroom cabinet where she kept her make-up and opened the door. She was going to present an image as cool and remote as anything Clay projected tonight, even if it killed her.

He thought she was a shrewd, tough businesswoman who'd had men galore and had an eye to the main chance. Fine. Better that than him finding out the truth—that she hadn't dated in months and was that singularly incongruous anomaly, a twenty-eight-year-old virgin. Wouldn't he just love that!

The last thought raised her head and brought her eyes narrowing. Clay was the enemy. As long as she remembered that, everything would be all right.

She closed the door behind her and began to climb the stairs...

CHAPTER FOUR

'TOPEKA'S? Have you booked a table?'

As Clay's Aston Martin drew up outside the restaurant and nightclub half of London would give their eye teeth to enter, Robyn spoke without thinking. Anyone who was anyone was seen at Topeka's. It was the in place, the buzz of the metropolis, and there was nothing so sordid as prices on the menus. If one could afford to be seen in Topeka's one could afford to pick up the tab, and as the clientele read like an excerpt from *Who's Who* there was never a problem.

'There'll be a table.' The words hadn't left his lips before the doorman was at the car, all ingratiating smiles, saying, 'So nice to see you again, Mr Lincoln,' as he ushered them inside.

Robyn saw Clay slip him the keys to the car along with a folded twenty-pound note, and her eyes widened. It was common knowledge just a few privileged customers had their own parking spots in the basement of the building; she might have known Clay would be one of them. Was he showing off? Trying to impress her? Emphasising he could afford to buy Brett PR a thousand times over?

She cast a sidelong glance at him from under her eye-lashes, and as she did so the head waiter emerged like a genie out of a lamp at their side. Again he was all teeth and bows and, although the exalted interior seemed full to Robyn, within moments they were seated at a table for two at the edge of the dance floor. A prestigious spot of course, she thought waspily.

She tried not to stare but it was hard. There were at least three celebrities within spitting distance—not that anything so coarse could possibly occur in Topeka's, Robyn thought wryly—and several more scattered round the room in which diamonds and Diors mingled with Guccis and Armanis in a blatant display of unlimited wealth. Never mind that some of the women present were on their third face-lift and dressed in clothes more suited to someone half their age, which they had starved their bodies to fit by the look of them—all that mattered was that they were here, now, where they could see and be seen.

The opulent surroundings, glittering diners and expectant buzz in the air *were* heady, Robyn admitted to herself, as a thrill of excitement vied with the butterflies doing a flamenco in her stomach. And Clay was used to this all the time. It was a different world. She was in Clay Lincoln territory now.

As her eyes returned to Clay, the intensity of his expression unnerved her, and foolishly she said the first thing that came into her head and was a follow-up from her last thoughts. 'Do you come here often?'

As soon as it was out she realised it was the oldest cliché in the world and blushed furiously, the more so when she could see quite well he was trying not to smile. 'Fairly often.' He settled back in his chair, perfectly relaxed and at ease. 'Surprisingly, for these sort of places, they have an excellent chef who does the best seafood in London. The tempura king scallops with sweet chili sauce have to be tasted to be believed. All too often a place gets a reputation simply because some of the so-called beautiful people frequent it, and the food's abysmal.'

'And of course you wouldn't be guilty of ever going anywhere just for the kudos,' Robyn said with a tartness that surprised her before she fell silent, secretly ashamed of herself.

He remained perfectly still, staring at her until the colour which had just begun to subside returned with fresh vigour. That had been catty, Robyn acknowledged with silent misery, and she just wasn't like that, not normally. What was it in Clay that brought out the very worst in her? 'I'm sorry, that wasn't very nice,' she said quietly after taking a deep breath for courage. 'Especially when you've brought me to such a wonderful place to eat. It's no business of mine where you go or what you do.'

'I've had worse things said to me in my time,' Clay said drily. 'But to answer your question...' he sat up, leaning forward slightly and fixing her in the silver light of his eyes '...perhaps when I was younger I might have done what you suggested. It helped to play the game then; it was important in the business sense as well as socially. Now? No, I don't think so. I choose where I go and who I want to be with very carefully, and purely for my own satisfaction.'

'Oh.' As always she had underestimated him and he had managed to completely take the ground from under her feet. She wasn't at all sure if he had paid her a compliment or not for a start. Her stomach muscles tightened and she was never so pleased to see anyone as when the head waiter appeared at the table in the next instant with the cocktails Clay had ordered.

'Non-alcoholic for you, Mr Lincoln? You're driving I take it?' the man said genially with another beaming smile.

'Just so, Charles,' Clay returned with an easy nod.

They appeared to be on very good terms. Robyn accepted her own drink with a smile of thanks, and took a sip—finding it delicious and very definitely alcoholic!—

before she glanced down at the menu which had been placed in front of her when they'd first been seated. It was written in English, German, French, Italian and what looked like Japanese, but she found most of the English terms incomprehensible so it wasn't much help. What was Dover sole meunière when it was at home for a start? Or chicken salmagundi? Or roast langoustine with mango salsa?

'Too much choice, isn't there?'

As she raised her eyes and looked into Clay's face she just knew he was aware of her predicament.

'Perhaps you would let me choose my favourites for you?' he continued smoothly, the head waiter at his elbow. 'I can thoroughly recommend the smoked ham linguini for starters.'

She nodded in what she hoped was a cool, languid, cosmopolitan sort of way. 'Thank you.'

'The linguini, then, Charles, with perhaps the tempura king scallops to follow. And I seem to remember the white chocolate *crème brûlée* with pineapple was particularly good last time. Do you have any of that tonight?'

'For you, Mr Lincoln, I will make it myself. I will make sure it is on the dessert menu,' the waiter said effusively.

'Many thanks, Charles.'

Did he actually like such fawning? Robyn took another sip of the vivid blue cocktail as the man whipped the menus away and then raised her gaze again to Clay's. The crystal eyes were waiting for her. 'It's expected by most of the clients, Robyn,' he said as though she had spoken the criticism out loud.

'Sorry?' She couldn't believe he'd read her mind *again*.

'It's part of the illusion,' he continued quietly. 'Some people need it; it's their security, their assurance that they are in control and important, that they're impregnable.'

She gave up trying to pretend. 'I think that's very sad,' she said slowly. 'Don't you?' Because he wasn't like that. She didn't know how she knew, she just suddenly knew she did know.

He shrugged, the hard face closed and giving nothing away. 'Whatever helps you sleep at night,' he said levelly. The light above them was slanting across his face, picking out the tiny lines radiating from the corners of his eyes and his mouth and catching the odd gleam of silver in the ebony hair. But none of it detracted from his appeal; in fact the signs of maturity which hadn't been there all those years ago added an extra dimension to the lethal attractiveness. It was a cynical face, made all the more devastating by the rugged sophistication that sat on him so easily and was a product of unlimited wealth.

What would it be like to smooth those lines away? To kiss the cynicism from that chiselled mouth and watch it mellow and soften under warm caresses? He'd felt wonderful all those years ago.

As soon as the thought was there Robyn was horrified, her head dropping immediately as she sought to hide her shock.

'What's the matter?' He'd been watching her closely.

'Nothing.' Thank goodness he hadn't been privy to that thought!

'Meaning you don't intend to tell me.'

'Exactly,' she confirmed coolly as she raised her eyes to his.

He was grinning when she looked at him again and it did the weirdest things to her equilibrium. 'I blame the red hair,' he drawled mildly.

'What?' She knew exactly what he meant but wasn't about to say so.

'But who could complain about such beauty?' he said silkily.

He was flirting with her, creating a mood. She stared at him warily, trying to prevent every muscle in her body from turning to water. 'This is ridiculous,' she said weakly. 'Us being here like this. Cass should never have involved you.'

'Ah, now you've brought it up, my proposition. Don't you want to hear what I've got to say? If nothing else, that's businesslike.' He tilted his head, surveying her mockingly.

Was he laughing at her? She stiffened, frowning slightly as she said, 'I thought I'd made myself clear on that score.'

'I'm willing to finance another assistant, two if the situation calls for it, but clearly there would be more to it than that.' It was as though she hadn't spoken. 'We would need to get down to basic facts and figures—Cassie was somewhat vague—but the way I see it...' He continued talking for some minutes, his tone cool and steady and matter-of-fact, and Robyn found herself listening to him with growing excitement. She tried to quell it, she really, really tried, but the future he was dangling so tantalisingly was like forbidden fruit—overwhelmingly tempting.

'Of course all this would depend on my accountant looking over your accounts and so on, but I don't foresee a problem there. Do you?' Clay finished just as the waiter brought their first course. 'I'm sure everything is in order.'

'I... But—'

'I said a sleeping partner and I meant it, Robyn. My people would need to see certain details on a regular basis, but I have more than enough to do than interfere in your business.'

The wine waiter was hovering with the wine Clay had

ordered and, once they were alone again, Robyn took a deep breath and said steadily, 'Why, Clay? Why would you be prepared to help me like this? Are you that friendly with Cass and Guy?'

'I see them rarely but I count them as good friends, besides which—if I can be crass—the amount I'm talking about here is not going to be missed quite frankly.' His tone was almost apologetic.

She nodded. She could believe that certainly. It was just the thought that she would be beholden to Clay Lincoln, in his debt for sure, that was hard to come to terms with. And it was only in that moment she acknowledged silently to herself that she was seriously considering his offer, the realisation causing her to choke momentarily on a piece of pasta.

Suicide. Mental and emotional suicide one little part of her brain warned fiercely. No—he'd *said* he wouldn't be around, that he had no intention of getting involved, the other part argued persuasively. He'd make this offer, set the ball rolling and then hand it over to his minions and that would be the end of that as far as he was concerned.

But this was *Clay*. She hated him, she had done so for years. So what? that other voice said with silky reason. What had that to do with business? This was something quite separate from feelings.

She took several gulps of wine to dislodge the pasta and tried to get a grip on herself. As far as Clay was concerned this was an easy answer to a request from Cass and Guy; as he'd intimated, the amount he'd put into the business—although massive to her—was a drop in the ocean to him. It would have been a deal made in heaven, the sort of thing that only happens once in a lifetime in the rat race of the business world, if only—and the if was huge—it had been someone other than Clay making the offer.

During the course of the meal several distinguished personalities stopped at their table and exchanged a few words with Clay. He was always careful to introduce her and everyone was very polite, but more than once—especially where the female of the species was concerned—Robyn had the feeling their thoughts ran along the line of, What is he doing with *her*? Or perhaps she was just paranoid? But she didn't think so.

The meal was as delicious as Clay had promised and by unspoken mutual consent they concentrated on the good food, Clay's conversation being as light and amusing as though this were an actual date.

Robyn didn't want to enjoy herself but it grew progressively hard not to. They finished the meal with a selection of cheeses and coffee and by now the dim lighting, sexy background music and general atmosphere of intimacy ephasised the fact that she was sitting opposite a twenty-four-carat male sex-bomb. He'd always had it—that undefinable something impossible to pin down but which had made certain men millions on the silver screen—but with added maturity the magnetic quality had enhanced a hundredfold.

'Shall we dance?'

'What?' It was a squawk and she was instantly sixteen again, all the gloss and hard-won confidence of the intervening years swept away with just three words.

Her breath caught in her throat as she watched Clay rise to his feet, his mouth curved in a smile and his eyes glittering as he held out his hand to her. She couldn't do anything else but stand up; it would have been unthinkable to leave him standing there in full view of everyone. Even Clay Lincoln didn't deserve that. Besides... Her throat went dry as her traitorous brain ruthlessly pointed out the truth. She wanted to know what it felt like to be in his arms, to be held close to him. She had never danced with him, after all.

For the first time in her life she knew what it was to have legs of jelly as they moved out onto the small dance floor, Clay's warm hand at her elbow. And then he turned her to face him and took her into his arms and her senses exploded.

It was a good job he didn't expect her to speak because conversation was quite beyond her at that moment, but as it was he merely drew her against him, his fingers splaying on the small of her back as her hands hesitantly rested on his upper arms. He felt and smelt so good—too good, she warned herself.

You're twenty-eight years old, running your own business, successful, worldly. She kept repeating the words over and over in her mind as they drifted round the floor until her racing heartbeat and the feeling that she was a naïve schoolgirl who didn't know her left foot from her right began to fade. The trouble was the last few years of relentlessly hard work and effort had meant that even the limited social life she'd had before she'd started her own business had been curtailed, and after the devastating experience with Clay she had never felt really confident of her own attractiveness to the opposite sex.

She had adopted a somewhat distant façade, one of cool friendliness as self-protection, and although she could function beautifully in her chosen career and project a boldness and self-assurance in her work and dealings with clients and contacts, Robyn the woman kept very much in her shell. But now that shell was being rattled...

'Your hair smells of apple blossom.' His voice was low

and throaty and she had to clench her stomach muscles in order not to betray the quiver it produced.

'Does it?' As sparkling repartee it wasn't much, but Robyn was just glad her voice sounded fairly normal when every nerve in her body was in hyperdrive.

'You've grown into a very beautiful woman, Robyn, but then, many men must have told you that.'

'A few.' She managed to inject a laughing lightness into her tone now and was inordinately pleased with herself. Okay, so he might be the sexiest thing since sliced bread, and she had no doubt every female between sixteen and sixty in London would love to be where she was right now, but he was just a little too sure of himself! One click of his fingers and he expected the females to line up, did he? Well, not this one. No way, no how. And that held, whatever happened businesswise.

'Cassie thinks you should relax more.' One strong hand lifted her chin, his eyes holding hers easily with their penetrating silver light, and again the full impact of his handsomeness swept over her, causing her to groan silently inside. He was just too damn gorgeous to be real, that was for sure, and it wasn't *fair*...

'My sister worries too much,' Robyn said with a note of dryness in her voice. If Cass had regaled him with stories of her non-existent social life she wouldn't be responsible for her actions when she saw Cass next. 'If it's not Guy or the twins, then it's me. She'll be better when the baby arrives; she didn't stop fussing over the twins for months—every squeak or cry had her up and running. I love her like mad but when the twins were first born it was the most peaceful few months I'd ever had. She's a great mum, though,' she added quickly in case he thought her words were ones of criticism. 'Absolutely the best.'

'You've never felt the inclination to settle down yourself?' he asked quietly, the subtle spicy scent of his aftershave teasing her senses. How was it that on some men aftershave just smelt like aftershave, and on others it turned into something so sexy and intoxicating that it ought to have a warning label? Robyn asked herself weakly, merely shaking her head in answer to his question. She wasn't inclined to go down that road.

'Not even been tempted?' he persisted softly.

What was this? The third degree? She stiffened slightly, moving back in his arms as a dart of annoyance hit. Every instinct was warning her the less Clay knew about her the better but she wasn't quite sure why. She didn't for one moment think he would be interested in her—it wasn't that—but he was the type of man who would file things away in that formidable computer he called a brain and use them against her in the future.

Future? She tensed further. Why on earth was she linking the words future and Clay Lincoln together in any way, shape or form? She couldn't let herself accept his offer; it was out of the question. It had to be. All the danger signals were at red.

'Why do I get the sudden feeling I'm holding a board in my arms?' It was cool and faintly amused, and hit Robyn on the raw like nothing else could have done.

This was just a game to him, an entertaining diversion for an hour or two. They stared at each other, Clay's gaze faintly quizzical and Robyn's brown eyes dilated with bitterness and hurt. And then she turned her head, gazing over his shoulder coolly.

'Who has made you hate men the way you do?' Clay asked very softly. 'Because you do, don't you?'

She jerked back in his arms as though she had been stung, her face shocked. 'Don't be ridiculous,' she said sharply. 'I don't hate men.' Not ninety-nine per cent of them anyway, just one particular man. Although she couldn't very well go into that!

'Cassie thinks there was someone,' the relentlessly soft voice continued quietly, his eyes never leaving her face for a second. 'She says you've never talked about it but she suspects a boy at university, or someone you met shortly after you left there? She thinks someone hurt you badly, Robyn.'

Robyn's mind had been whirling in an agony of desperate humiliation, but suddenly she realised he was being completely frank. She'd suspected at first his remark was a lead-up to the way they had parted all those years ago, but now she saw he really didn't have the faintest idea he'd been the one to break her heart and send her emotions into a deep freeze.

She gave a frosty little smile. 'Like I said earlier, Cass thinks too much at times,' she said evenly, her voice belying the hot colour in her cheeks. 'Anyway, at Guy's party you accused me of being some sort of *femme fatale* who wouldn't be averse to using her body to get what or where she wanted. That doesn't sound like someone who doesn't like men.'

'Ah, but I've had a chat with Cassie and Guy since then,' Clay said with total unconcern at her outraged face. 'And before you accuse me of further crimes, might I add that they did all the chatting with no provocation from me. Not that I didn't find it interesting,' he added thoughtfully.

'Oh, I'm so glad you weren't bored,' she said with acid sarcasm, although the fact that she was so close to that big, male body and her hands—resting as they were against the hard wall of his chest—could feel the steady beat of his heart brought a slight breathlessness to her voice she could have done without. It spoke of weakness and she couldn't afford that with Clay.

'Bored talking about you?' The silver eyes narrowed. 'I don't think that's possible. Whatever else you are—and I haven't decided on that yet—you certainly aren't boring, Robyn Brett. You weren't as a child either. Irritating on occasion, especially when you insisted on following Cassie and the rest of us everywhere and throwing a paddy if you were sent home, but never boring.'

The only times she had ever tagged onto Cass were when Clay was around, but fortunately he didn't know that. Robyn steeled herself to change tack before this conversation got out of hand. It was too emotionally fraught—at least on her side—and that wasn't good. She needed to be cool and composed around Clay, and although she didn't feel it she could at least pretend.

She could feel her heart racing, a frantic, fast thud that made her light-headed and giddy, but she gave no sign of her inward agitation when she said, her voice light now, even teasing, 'Careful, Clay, or you'll be guilty of giving me a compliment and that would never do.' She arched her eyebrows mockingly.

'A cute change of subject.' He smiled slowly, and she could feel the impact singing down her spine. 'So, you don't want to talk about him, right? Okay, I get the message.'

'If there was a him; no, I don't.'

'No problem. I don't like post-mortems either.' He increased his pressure on the small of her back, drawing her into him again as easily as if she were thistledown. One hand remained warm and firm against her spine and the other lifted to stroke the silky smooth skin of her face in a light, caressing gesture that she had to warn herself not to react to. 'Your skin's incredible, do you know that?'

he whispered softly, almost to himself. 'So creamy and soft.'

She wasn't going to play this dangerous game. Robyn ignored the frissons of pleasure circulating in her bloodstream and managed to say carefully, 'I wasn't hinting for compliments a minute ago, Clay,' as she kept her body from relaxing.

'What?' And then as he understood he made a small male sound of irritation deep in his throat. 'Hell, I know that: stop being so damn prickly.'

She didn't like the accusation but at least the intimate mood he'd woven so expertly had been shattered; in fact he was frowning at her now she noticed wryly. She took no notice of the little ache of regret and said brightly, 'My mistake.'

Clay was looking at her in a way that made her wonder what he was thinking. 'I have the strangest feeling you're not a lady that makes mistakes,' he said thoughtfully. 'And you really don't like me, do you!' It was a statement, not a question, and said with the faintest underlying note of surprise.

Had she managed to prick that inflated male ego just the tiniest bit? Robyn asked herself silently. She hoped so. Oh, she did so hope so. 'Is that part of the deal? Liking you?' she asked with outrageous audacity. 'You didn't make that clear earlier.'

The frown deepened; in fact he was positively scowling now and his voice was flat and edged with anger when he said, 'If you're suggesting what I think you are suggesting I am more than capable of getting female company without having to buy it.'

'I wouldn't have dreamed of suggesting such a thing,' Robyn said sweetly. 'I'm sure you're capable of attracting most women.'

'Thank you,' Clay murmured drily. 'Thank you so much.'

For once he wasn't having it all his own way and it felt great, Robyn admitted with a touch of ruefulness. It probably shouldn't matter so much and she shouldn't get such pleasure from his obvious disquiet, but she just couldn't help it and that was that. He shouldn't have tried flirting with her!

When the music finished in the next moment he escorted her back to the table without suggesting another dance, and for the next hour or so that they remained at the nightclub he didn't ask her to dance again. They talked business most of the time and Robyn realised Clay had taken it for granted that she would accept his offer. It brought temptation to the fore again.

And why not? the little voice in her head argued persuasively. She couldn't have made it clearer tonight how she felt—his own words were witness to that—so if he wanted to put up some cash and was content to leave her to carry on as she had been doing for the last few years, why not take advantage of the situation? One thing was for sure, backers like Clay Lincoln were a once-in-a-lifetime opportunity for a little business like hers. Drew would think she was crazy to turn such a break down.

But how often would she have to meet up with him? Would it all be done through his team of accountants or would it necessitate face-to-face contact now and again? She pondered how to ask the question but there wasn't really an easy way, so she took a deep breath and just said it as it was.

His thick black lashes masked his expression as he looked down into the glass of mineral water he had poured himself after just one glass of wine, but he responded with barely a pause, his voice even and expressionless as he said, 'Like I said, Robyn, I have more than enough on my plate than to interfere with your work. Contact would be minimal.'

It didn't really answer her question but she knew she had pushed that particular avenue as far as she could go, and when all was said and done—and for whatever reason he was being so generous, whether it was his friendship with Guy or what—all the gain was on her side.

With the contacts she had made recently and the work she knew she could acquire given the extra funding, she couldn't really lose on this. Everything to gain and nothing to lose in fact.

But did anything ever come that easy? His gaze rose again and she saw his face was cool and distant, the silver eyes more wintery than ever. He'd clearly given up on the evening, she thought soberly, refusing to acknowledge any shred of regret in the multitude of feelings flooding her chest. The little dalliance he'd allowed himself hadn't turned out as amusing as he'd thought, and now that ruthless mind had slotted her away as not worth bothering about. Too much hassle. Whatever.

In spite of the beautiful surroundings filled with London's cream of the beautiful people, Robyn wasn't sorry to leave the nightclub a few minutes later. Her nerves were so sensitised they were painful, and she had a funny little ache in her heart region she didn't care to examine.

She needed the sanctuary of her home as never before, her haven where she could close the door and shut the rest of the world out. Ridiculously the thought of her little house made her want to cry, and it horrified her. Whatever was the matter with her? There was absolutely no need to be so emotional, she chided herself silently as the Aston

Martin appeared like magic as she and Clay exited the building. Everything was fine.

'So...' The car was weaving through the streets, shiny and wet after a sudden shower, when Clay spoke at the side of her. 'I'll set things up tomorrow morning before I leave for the States, okay? Contact Mike Robinson on this number—' he reached into the breast pocket of his leather jacket and extracted a card '—and he'll talk you through everything.'

His voice was quiet and even, expressionless almost, although Robyn thought she detected a slightly bored note now. She bit her lip hard. She hadn't actually verbalised her agreement to the offer but it was probably best all round that she didn't continue to make a big deal of this. 'All right, Clay, and thank you. I appreciate this.' She tried to match his tone but failed miserably. 'It's very generous of you.'

'I could tell that really hurt.'

'What?' She turned to stare at the dark profile.

'No matter,' he drawled cryptically.

Annoying man. 'Look, Clay, if you're regretting the offer—'

'Not at all. This whole evening has been rather an...interesting experience.' He had cut her off before she could continue, his voice slightly mocking.

Robyn wasn't into enigmatic statements. If nothing else she was a plain-spoken, straightforward girl, she thought crossly, her words reflecting her thoughts as she said flatly, 'Interesting? And what does that mean exactly? Are we talking in a patronising sense here by any chance?'

'Give me strength.' It was the quality of his voice, rather than the volume, that told her he wasn't quite so calm and remote as he'd like her to believe. They had just arrived at the top of Robyn's street, and now Clay sped

with—in Robyn's eyes—unnecessary speed down the road, whisking the car into a parking space in front of Robyn's Fiesta and cutting the engine with uncalled for violence. 'You have to be the most infuriating, difficult female I've had the misfortune to come into contact with for years,' he ground out tightly into the screaming silence that followed. 'Hell, I've gone the extra mile for you—'

For Cass and Guy's sake, yeah, right, Robyn thought tensely, determined not to acknowledge he had a point.

'And you've done nothing but be a pain in the—' He stopped abruptly, running a hand through his hair in a gesture that spoke of intense frustration. 'Can't you just be normal?' he asked furiously. 'Why does everything have to be such a damn confrontation? Don't you ever loosen up and relax a bit? It's not that hard and you might even find you enjoy it.'

'Being with you, you mean?' She shot the words back. 'Because that is what this is all about at root level, isn't it? The great Clay Lincoln, God's gift to womankind, is annoyed because he's met one female who hasn't fallen down and instantly worshipped at the shrine.'

He stared at her as if she was mad. Perhaps she *was* mad, Robyn thought with bitter rage. Certainly the cool, calm façade she had been determined to adopt earlier had been blown apart. And it was all his fault! Arrogant, supercilious man that he was. He was a million times worse than he'd been all those years ago.

And then, as she glared into the dark handsome face and he glared back, silver eyes caught with brown and everything suddenly became very still. Robyn was conscious of certain outward things: the smell of rich leather from the car's interior and the faint whiff of the aftershave her senses had picked up earlier; a dog barking somewhere in the distance; the sound of a car as it passed them.

But the only real things in the universe were the metallic eyes holding hers.

And they weren't cold or remote any longer.

She waited breathlessly for his touch and when his hand lifted and touched her cheek in the lightest of caresses she remained absolutely still, her heart beating so hard it hurt. His flesh was warm, and as he moved forwards, drawing her towards him, she didn't resist. She couldn't have resisted.

Their mouths met and she softened against him; she couldn't help it. His lips were persuasive and knowing and the cosy cocoon within the car intoxicatingly intimate. The kiss went on and on in ever increasing spirals of pleasure, and now there was something hotter and sharper at the base of it that had Robyn wanting to be even closer to him. She wanted to run her hands over his hard body, to feel it pressing against her, to know every inch of him. To taste and feel and touch naked flesh.

The lasciviousness of her thoughts stabbed awareness into the tide of pleasure and she wrenched her mouth from his, sinking back into her own seat, her body trembling. This was crazy, *crazy*. One moment she was telling him she didn't want anything to do with him and the next she'd fallen into his arms like a ripe peach. And where had that last thought come from?

It had started to rain again outside the warm confines of the car and now the raindrops pattered on the roof, running in rivulets down the windscreen as Robyn stared straight ahead. She didn't dare look at Clay.

She waited for the mocking remark she was sure would come, some cool, sardonic comment on her inconsistency, but when Clay did speak it was only to say huskily, 'I'll see you to the door,' before he slid out of the car and walked round the bonnet to open the passenger door. The old-fashioned courtesy was an integral part of him but her stomach muscles bunched as she took his proffered hand and joined him on the pavement.

Did he expect to be asked in to continue what they had begun in the car? she asked herself as they moved hastily to the steps of the house which were separated from the pavement by three feet of paved front garden behind small iron railings.

She glanced up at him as they reached the bottom step, her eyes huge. And, if so, what was she going to do?

The raindrops made her blink and it was through a misty haze she watched Clay's face coming closer, and then their mouths were fused again and the rest of the world disappeared. The kiss was fierce and tender at the same time and it touched the quintessence of her being with its sweet potency. And then they had drawn apart and Robyn had no idea how long the embrace had lasted. All she knew was that now it was over she felt bereft.

She gulped for air, staring at him as he took a step backwards away from her. 'Don't forget to make that call,' he said thickly. 'I'll set it up for tomorrow.'

'Call?' He could have been talking in a foreign language.

'Mike. Mike Robinson.'

It took a moment or two but then she managed to say, 'No, no, I won't,' as her brain engaged again.

He nodded, and they looked at each other through the foot or so of space between them for what seemed like an eternity before he turned away, walking back to the car.

He was going. She stared after him, knowing she ought to turn and open the door rather than remain on the doorstep but it was as though brain and body were unconnected.

He raised a hand in brief salute before sliding into the car but she was incapable of responding to the casual gesture, and then the engine started and the car pulled out into the road before disappearing like a streak of lightning down the street. As though he couldn't wait to get away.

The last thought permeated the fog of her mind and she stiffened, her eyes widening. Oh, no, no, what had she done? Had she thrown herself at him again in a ghastly repeat of years ago? Had he felt obliged to kiss her in the car and then again on the doorstep because she had made it clear she was expecting it? Desiring it?

The little moan from deep within brought her fumbling for her key, and once inside the house she stumbled straight upstairs to the kitchen, switching on the kettle automatically. Coffee. Lots and lots of coffee to help her think. That potent cocktail and then the wine had clouded her senses and her judgement, that was it. She hugged the thought to her, drawing on it as her heart pounded alarmingly in her breast. That was all it was. She was just a bit tipsy.

She drank the first cup of coffee hot and black, and if nothing else the shot of adrenalin helped her face the fact that she was as sober as a judge. The problem here wasn't a momentary lapse due to alcohol; the problem was Clay Lincoln. She clenched her hands together and then purposefully forced herself to relax her fingers one by one before fixing another cup of coffee.

Had she invited him to kiss her? *Conscripted* it even? She played the tape over in her mind and took a big gulp of the burning liquid as the answer hit. He might well have thought so from the way she'd behaved. But there *had* been something there in the car when they'd looked at each other, something Clay had felt too...hadn't there? Or was she fooling herself?

She dragged in a deep swig of air and stared at the sculptured cream tiles on the wall. She hadn't wanted the kiss to end. She gave a little groan of humiliation. Something Clay Lincoln would have been only too aware of with his experience. No doubt he was congratulating himself this very minute that he had made her eat her words as soon as they were uttered. And it had been *him* who had drawn away, had taken a mental as well as a physical step backwards. History had a very nasty habit of repeating itself at times.

She straightened, willing herself not to cry nor shout nor scream. This was nothing, she had to get it into perspective. They'd exchanged a kiss, that was all, and now he was off to the States and she probably wouldn't see him again for another twelve years. And if she did, if this business venture caused their paths to cross some time in the months ahead, she'd make darn sure nothing like tonight was repeated.

When the telephone extension rang on the kitchen wall right at the side of her she nearly jumped out of her skin, and she grimaced at her jumpiness as she reached for the receiver. Cass no doubt, or Drew.

It was neither. 'Robyn?' Clay's voice was soft and deep and smoky, and her breath strangled in her throat. 'It's Clay.'

She made a noise that didn't sound like anything and then coughed once before she lied, 'Sorry, a mouthful of coffee went down the wrong way. Is anything the matter?'

'I was just ringing to say I'd like to do this evening again some time,' he said quietly. 'I'm back in the country in a few weeks so can I give you a call then?'

Her heart gave an odd, painful little jump but without him there in front of her it was easier to say, her voice firm, 'I don't think so, Clay. You're an extremely busy man and I've got more than enough on my plate, and if we're going to be business partners—'

'I'm only going to be your sleeping partner, Robyn.'

Why did he have to keep putting it like that? She blinked, pressing her lips tightly together for a second. 'Nevertheless, I don't believe in mixing business with—' she hesitated just the merest fraction of a moment '—my social life.'

'Pleasure, Robyn.' The dark voice was merciless. 'The word you're looking for is pleasure, and it has eight letters, not four. You can actually use it in polite company.'

She had been right, he was just loving this! Well, he could take a running jump... 'Whatever,' she snapped tartly. 'Goodnight, Clay.'

She replaced the receiver without waiting for a reply and then stared at it for a good thirty seconds, her heart racing. It was another thirty seconds before she realised she was willing him to ring again, and that realisation was enough to propel her out of the kitchen and into the bathroom, where she began to run herself a bath, her hands shaking.

She wasn't going to waste another thought on Clay Lincoln. It would be weeks before he was back in the country again, and if—by chance or design—their paths should cross then, she would have had plenty of time to have herself firmly under control.

CHAPTER FIVE

'So WHAT is it you're mad about exactly?' Cassie asked in the sort of soothingly patient tone she used with the children when they were being truculent for no good reason. 'All's well that ends well as far as I can see. You've got your backer, and one who's not likely to interfere with the business in any way, and now you can afford to take on extra staff and go for more work which is what you've been gagging to do for months.'

Robyn stared at her sister frustratedly, and then caught Guy's eye who was sitting at the side of Cassie at the kitchen table. He shrugged and then made a face that said eloquently, Leave it, Robyn. You aren't going to win this one and you know it, before he got up and beat a hasty retreat.

'Oh, *Cass*.' Robyn didn't know if she wanted to kiss her or hit her. 'You know what I'm mad about, now then. I told you not to say a word to Clay and you couldn't get to him fast enough. You put him in a difficult position as well as me.'

'Nonsense.' Cassie's voice was brisk. 'If Clay hadn't wanted to get involved wild horses wouldn't have dragged him to see you, I promise you. In all the time we've known Clay I've never known him to do anything he doesn't want to.'

'Cass, you blackmailed him with friendship,' Robyn stated grimly.

'Not at all. I merely mentioned a couple of relevant facts and then left it at that. There was no pressure from me for Clay to contact you,' Cassie said firmly. 'That was totally down to him.'

Guy had been right, she wasn't going to be able to convince Cassie she had acted out of turn, Robyn thought resignedly. Her sister had always had an extra portion of self-assurance and faith in herself which was positively daunting at times, but when married to Cassie's naturally warm heart and loving nature the end result was normally positive and healthy for those about her. Although this time Robyn wasn't too sure...

'Look, sis, if it makes you feel better I promise I won't say a word to anyone about anything to do with you or your business in the future. How about that?' Cassie beamed at her, and Robyn stifled an irritable sigh.

Cass knew full well she was shutting the stable door after the horse had bolted, but there was nothing she could do but accept the status quo and smile, Robyn acknowledged wearily. This was Cass—like it or lump it.

'I shall hold you to that.' Robyn's voice was stern but her face was indulgent. Cass meant well and she knew her sister loved her all the world which was why she couldn't resist meddling in her affairs. But it had to stop. She wasn't a kid any more.

'So...' Cassie checked the children were still playing happily in their sandpit just outside the kitchen door— something that made for a constantly gritty floor—and took a sip of her coffee '...what's been happening the last two weeks, then? You said on the phone Clay's set up the deal. Is it all finalised? Everything gone through all right?'

'Uh-huh.' Her workload had meant she hadn't visited her sister for a fortnight, and she couldn't really afford to be here now with the amount of paperwork waiting for her at home, but it was a beautiful Sunday morning and the sun had been shining and she hadn't been able to resist spending a couple of hours with her nephews who were at the stage where they seemed to grow every day. 'But I've come to have a break from work, not to talk about it,' she said with a smile to take the sting out of the words.

Cassie accepted the rebuke with her normal good humour. And after being persuaded to stay for lunch Robyn finally left mid afternoon for the short drive home. She had been coaxed into the sandpit by Jason and Luke, and now her hair was full of sand, her face was sticky from goodbye kisses from baby mouths smeared with ice-cream and lollipops, and her nose was sunburnt. But Robyn adored her small nephews and the hours with Cassie and her family had relaxed her.

So it was all the more of a shock when she drew up outside her house just as Clay's Aston Martin purred down the street. Robyn watched the car approach in horror and then glanced in the mirror over the windscreen. A grubby, rosy face devoid of make-up stared back at her, her hair—which was looped high on her head in a riotous pony-tail—completing the picture of someone half her age. Someone very like the kid sister of bygone years.

She groaned softly. Clad in her armour of well-groomed, cool career woman she had only just managed to hold her own with Clay; now she felt like a bird with one wing down. But it was too late to hide and certainly too late to go anywhere. He had drawn alongside her and was now indicating for her to wind down her window. His, she thought sourly as she leant across the passenger seat to oblige, would be electric—unlike hers.

'Are you going out or coming home?' Clay asked as she struggled with the window which always got stuck halfway and needed a good push.

She left it at half-mast and straightened, flushed and

dishevelled, and the caustic remark which had sprung to mind wasn't delivered with quite as much acidity as she would have liked when she took in the full impact of the dark tanned face, silver eyes and jet-black hair.

He's gorgeous. Her mind said it all by herself and in the circumstances it couldn't have been more unwelcome. Here was she, looking like something the cat wouldn't be seen dead dragging in, and here was Clay, the epitome of cool sophistication.

'I don't normally go out unwashed and filthy, funnily enough,' she said tightly, wishing she had bothered to put on a touch of mascara at least. She looked such a *mess*.

'Do I take it this is a bad moment?' he drawled mildly.

Bad moment? It couldn't be worse. 'Not really,' she lied with as much nonchalance as she could muster considering she could feel grains of sand in every crease and crevice of her body—some unmentionable—and was dying for a bath. 'I've just been round Cass's, that's all, and we've been playing in the sandpit.'

The raised eyebrows made her add hastily, her cheeks aglow, 'Me and the boys that is, Jason and Luke. Cass had a lie down after lunch and Guy had brought some work home, so I looked after the children for a bit. They— they like me to play with them.'

'Who enjoyed it the most? You or your nephews?' Clay asked softly, his eyes washing over the tumbled silky red-gold curls before coming to rest on her sun-tinted face.

At least it made her *sound* grown-up—the nephew bit— Robyn thought self-consciously, even if she didn't look it. 'We all did,' she managed flusteredly. 'They're smashing kids.' And then, when the silver gaze threatened to reduce her to babbling panic, she took a hold of herself and said steadily, 'I thought you were in the States? You said you wouldn't be back for a few weeks.'

'Back for a couple of days.' He made it sound as though he'd just popped down to the supermarket rather than come halfway across the world. 'I leave again the day after tomorrow.'

She nodded in what she hoped was a cool, I'm-not-at-all-impressed sort of way. 'Business?' she asked offhand-edly.

He shrugged dismissively. 'Not exactly.'

She waited, but when he wasn't more forthcoming, said carefully, 'Were you just passing or was this an actual visit? There isn't anything wrong with all the stuff I've given Mike, is there? He seemed to think everything was in order when we last spoke.'

'It's fine.' He hesitated, and for a second—just a split second—Robyn thought he was edgy, even nervous, be-fore she reminded herself this was Clay Lincoln and such words weren't even in his vocabulary. Not Clay's. 'I was calling to see if I could drag you away from your desk on such a beautiful summer's day.'

'I'm not at my desk,' she said quickly.

'So you aren't.' He smiled sexily.

'But I ought to be,' she said hastily, 'especially after being at Cass's all day, so I'm sorry but—'

'I don't intend to take no for an answer, Robyn.'

For a moment she thought she must have heard wrongly, but when she saw the sudden steely glint in the silver eyes her voice rose an octave or two as she said, 'I beg your pardon?'

'Like I said, I'm only back for a couple of days and there's a little job I'd like to talk to you about.'

'Oh, it's business.' The relief in her voice was trans-parent. 'You should have said. Will tomorrow do?' she suggested hopefully.

He smiled coolly, the narrowed gaze cold. 'Afraid not.'

'Oh.' She was disconcerted. And then, as she looked at him more closely and noticed the lines of tiredness around his mouth and eyes, she said quietly, 'When did you get back?'

'We touched down a couple of hours ago.'

'You must be exhausted, and you say you're leaving again tomorrow?' Whatever he'd come back for it must be important; perhaps that was what he was dealing with tomorrow.

He nodded, watching her closely. 'I thought we could combine our little talk with a meal somewhere,' he suggested evenly, 'before I go home and crash out for a few hours. What do you say?'

Another meal with Clay Lincoln? Another date that wasn't a date at all? Robyn's mind was racing. He'd virtually promised her there would be no contact once their business arrangement was set up. And then the more reasonable part of her mind cut in with, But he has got some sort of job in mind for me, and with his sort of contacts and influence I should at least listen to what it is. My business is still in the fledgling stage; I couldn't afford to let any opportunity pass me by.

But the thought of having to dress up and psyche herself up for another evening like the last one, with Clay holding all the cards as he lorded it in his own privileged world, did not appeal. Robyn made a split-second decision and said flatly, trying to keep all expression out of her voice, 'You're tired and you're hungry but, if you need to talk to me today, why not here? I can cook us something and then once we've had a chat you can go home and sleep and I can start work. I really do have masses to do.'

There was no visible change in his face or his body as he continued to look at her, but somehow, after a second or two, Robyn felt as though something had shifted, lightened. And then he said very formally, 'I don't want to put you to any trouble.'

'It's no trouble.' She didn't want him to get the wrong idea though, and so she added evenly, for extra emphasis, 'It will save us both time, won't it? I'm sure you're as busy as I am.'

He nodded slowly. 'Then, thank you, I accept.'

He had to drive down the street a little way for a parking space, and as the car drew away and disappeared Robyn leant back in her seat for a moment and let out her breath in a big whoosh. Was she being stupid? Should she just have refused to consider this job he knew about and have sent him on his way? But knowing Clay he wouldn't have gone anyway. She bit her lip hard.

The last two weeks had been a constant battle against letting him into her head every waking moment. The night hours she could do nothing about and he'd invaded her dreams relentlessly, and in ways that had made her go hot with embarrassment in the morning.

And now he was here, in the flesh. The last words caught at her senses and a flicker of something hot curled down her spine and into her lower stomach before she straightened, squaring her shoulders. Enough, enough of that, she warned herself grimly.

Nothing had changed. Nothing. Clay was still the same man who had rejected her so cruelly all those years ago, and she forgot that at her peril. He was ruthless and cold and cynical, a man without weakness who needed no one and lived his life totally on his own terms. He had been like that all those years ago under the skin although she hadn't realised it until Cass's wedding day, and he was more so now.

He had parked the Aston Martin and was walking up

the street towards her as she glanced in her mirror, and her heart started pounding with the force of a sledgehammer. He looked big, very big, the designer shirt and trousers he was wearing emphasising the muscled strength in his powerful, lean body as well as the aura of unlimited wealth. He was hard and handsome, an animal-like quality in each smooth stride, and sexy. Wildly, undeniably sexy. Oh, help...

She leant across and wound up the passenger window quickly, emerging from the car onto the pavement just before he reached her. It was only then that it dawned on her that the old jeans and sleeveless skinny top she had pulled on that morning had seen better days, and that the top in particular was a trifle too figure-hugging. It hadn't mattered at Cass's, but now...

As the silver eyes drifted across her breasts she could actually feel her nipples harden in response and she immediately turned to fumble with the lock of the car, babbling as she did so, 'I can do spaghetti Bolognese, or pork chops if you'd prefer? Or an omelette? That's about the limit of the choice I'm afraid.'

'Spaghetti Bolognese sounds great to me.'

It might sound great but she just hoped it tasted that way. Clay Lincoln was used to the best of everything and she was an adequate cook, no more. It was Cass who excelled in that department. But she couldn't go far wrong with spaghetti Bolognese—hopefully.

After locking the car she led the way into the house and up the stairs, aware she was trailing sand and wondering how big her bottom looked in the close-fitting jeans.

'Look, I really do need to have a quick bath.' Once on the top floor she turned to face him again. 'Would you like a glass of wine while you wait, or perhaps a long, cold drink? There's beer, or lemonade or something?' she added over her shoulder.

She had walked over to the windows leading onto the balcony on the last words, and now she opened them to let the warm summer breeze flow in as Clay said behind her, 'A beer sounds even better than the spaghetti Bolognese but I'm afraid I'm American in my preference for them cold straight from the fridge. I've never been able to understand the English desire for luke-warm beer,' he added with an apologetic grin that sent her hormones racing.

'Most people like them cold,' Robyn said quickly. 'I think it's only the older generation like my father who think it's sacrilege to chill beer.'

He nodded slowly. 'Perhaps it's because I can remember endless gallons of the warm stuff when I was a kid. The first time I ever tasted beer was a family party when we sneaked a few bottles and hid in the potting shed. At ten years of age it was pretty potent stuff and we drank it like pop. We were well and truly loaded, and boy, did we learn the hard way.'

He had been faintly smiling, but then, as Robyn said, 'We?' the smile died. She stared at him, wondering what she'd said.

'My brother and I,' he said shortly.

She couldn't hide her surprise, her eyes widening. 'I didn't know you've got a brother?' she said, searching her mind. He had never brought a brother along in the old days and she couldn't remember Cass or Guy ever mentioning one.

'Had.' It was terse. 'He's dead.'

'Oh, I'm sorry, Clay.' She was horrified at her innocent blunder and it must have shown, because the closed expression on his face softened a little.

He shrugged wearily, walking over to stand beside her and looking out over the rooftops into the blue sky above as he said quietly, 'There was an accident when we were eleven. Mitch...Mitch was my twin brother. We were very close.'

'How terrible for you.' She didn't know what to say. Why hadn't Guy or Cass ever mentioned it? Did they know?

And then she had her answer as Clay said flatly, 'It was a long time ago and I never talk about it. Or think about it.'

He was lying. As she looked at the hard profile she knew he was lying. He thought about it all right; whatever had happened had affected him so deeply he still found it difficult to talk about it. She knew she ought to leave it at that—he couldn't have made it plainer without being rude that he didn't want to discuss it—but this was the first time she felt she was seeing something of the real man inside the outward persona of wealthy playboy and ruthless business tycoon. 'Were you injured too?' she asked carefully. 'In the accident?'

'No.' The abruptness was painful rather than caustic, and Robyn could feel the darkness inside him. 'I wasn't with him at the time.' He stepped out onto the balcony, which was too tiny to take more than one small cane chair along with the tubs of flowers, lifting his face to the sunshine as he said, 'This is very pleasant. I can imagine you curling up out here with a good book.'

'That'll be the day!' She spoke lightly, knowing he needed to change the subject although she was intensely curious about his brother. 'I keep promising myself I'll have a day or even a few days of doing nothing, a holiday of sorts, but somehow it never happens. It's one of the things Cass reminds me about often,' she added wryly.

Her forbearance was rewarded by one of his rare smiles as he turned to face her again. Her heart turned over and she forced herself not to visibly react. 'She can be like a dog with a bone,' he agreed softly, adding immediately, 'but a very gentle, loving dog of course.'

'Of course.' Keep it light, Robyn. Light and easy. She took a small step backwards, waving at the chair as she said, 'Sit down and I'll bring you your drink. You can soak up a few rays while I freshen up.'

'I wouldn't dream of it. You're just as tired as me if not more, if you've been with Jason and Luke for any length of time. I'll come with you for the drink. I presume the beer is in the fridge in the kitchen?' he asked easily.

The beer *was* in the fridge in the kitchen, but she wanted him sitting up here, immobile, under control. He was too male, too virile, too much of everything just to be allowed to wander about! Tethered she could just about cope with him here.

She recognised the absurdity of her thoughts even as they entered her brain, but it didn't make them any less real or change the fluttering in her stomach.

'No, really, you relax,' she said quickly. 'It's no trouble.'

'I will relax.' It was very even and reasonable but the thread of steel was back. 'Once I have my beer I will return to this very spot, okay? I'm not into peeping through keyholes if that's what you're worried about.'

She stared at him, mortified. She was about to speak, to challenge him, but then common sense warned her that she wouldn't even stand a chance of winning this one. And twin brother or no twin brother Clay was still an arrogant pig! Whatever had happened in his past she still loathed him, she *did*. She did. The reiteration still wasn't as convincing as she would have liked. She stared at him a moment more and then admitted defeat.

'Please yourself,' she said a touch tartly.

'I will, Robyn.'

She didn't doubt that for a minute. Pleasing himself was a criterion men like Clay lived by. The waspishness of the thought was strangely comforting, fuelling, as it did, her determination to keep in mind that he was the enemy.

Once in the kitchen she poured the beer into a glass despite Clay's protestation he would drink it from the bottle, and then flounced immediately into the bathroom. He could sit on the balcony, he could sit in the sitting room, he could sit and watch her in the bath if he so desired! It really wouldn't affect her one way or the other what he did, because *he* didn't affect her. She wouldn't let him.

It was sheer heaven to divest herself of the sand, and once she had bathed she washed her hair too before climbing out of the bath and wrapping the bath sheet round her body sarong-style. Clean and scrubbed she felt more herself again.

She opened the door cautiously but all was quiet, and she padded through to the bedroom where she applied body lotion with reckless abandon on her arms which had also caught the sun, and then rich moisturing cream on her neck and face. Her nose was glowing like a beacon. She peered at herself in the mirror and groaned softly. Come home, Rudolph; all is forgiven, she thought wryly. A touch of make-up was definitely called for here.

Foundation cream toned down the redness to a warm glow, and she used just the merest stroke of mascara to enhance her lashes. She didn't want him to think she had made up for him. She had, but she didn't want him to think it!

After grabbing a pair of cotton combat trousers from

the wardrobe and a black vest-top, she dried her hair as quickly as she could and piled it up high on top of her head in a loose pony-tail. She was going for casual. Non-dressy, non-girly, non…come-on. Okay, so the vest top showed her figure off somewhat…satisfactorily, and the mass of burnished curls high on her head was a subtle contrast to the vest and combat trousers, but that wasn't her fault, was it?

She looked at herself in the mirror just as she was leaving the bedroom. Silver studs in her ears? Yes. A feminine touch without being too obvious. And a dab of perfume at her wrists and throat was just womanly, that was all.

She took a long, deep breath before she emerged out onto the landing, and then walked steadily over to the stairs and ran lightly up them after extracting another beer from the fridge. 'Reinforcements?' she called brightly as she saw Clay sitting on the balcony.

'Great, thanks.' He turned and smiled at her, but then his gaze returned almost immediately to the view as he said, 'Amazing what a bird's-eye view can reveal. Did you know the girl in the house opposite likes to sunbathe in the nude?'

Oh, no—she'd forgotten about Maria's little penchant for displaying herself to half of Kensington. The exotic dancer in one of the local nightclubs was a dedicated naturist as her perfect tan confirmed.

'Uh-huh,' she said nonchalantly.

'I'm beginning to think I miss a lot by living in Windsor.' He turned and added, 'Want any help with the meal?'

Robyn forced a thin smile. 'I wouldn't dream of dragging you away from the view,' she said pithily.

'I prefer the one I'm looking at now.' His voice was

soft, throaty, and it flustered her more than she would have liked.

She tried to think of something airy and blasé to say but her mind was blank. Completely blank. Come on, Robyn, you can do better than this, she warned herself silently. He's used to witty social chit-chat, light flirting and innuendo; that was the name of the game in the cosmopolitan circles Clay moved in. Someone staring gormlessly at him with their mouth half open was *not* his scene.

'Clay, what's this job you talked about?' she asked abruptly.

'Ah…' He stood up slowly, moving off the balcony and into the sitting room before continuing, his eyes on her flushed face, 'It won't be for a while yet.'

'A while?' There was something in his voice that made her wary.

'Next year…probably.' He eyed her unrepentantly.

'There isn't a job, is there?' she stated tightly.

'No,' he agreed meekly, 'although there probably will be. I'm sure opportunities will arise—'

'I don't want your handouts, Clay,' she snapped testily, 'and I don't appreciate being lied to.'

'It wasn't exactly a lie, more an exaggeration.'

'It was a lie, Clay.' Her voice brooked no argument.

'Okay, it was a lie.' He managed to look magnificently sexy and little-boy ingenuous at the same time. 'Does this mean no Bolognese?' he asked humbly.

'It should.' She didn't trust the humility. Such an emotion was an enigma to Clay Lincoln. But if there was no job prospect, it must mean he had come to see her because he wanted to and, despite every sane and sensible instinct that was urging her to show him the door, Robyn found herself saying, 'But as you're clearly dead on your feet I

can't exactly send you away hungry. But once you've
eaten, that's it. I've got work to do.'

'Thank you, Robyn.' It was far too humble to be gen-
uine.

Yes, right, thank you, Robyn. She was already berating
herself for being such an idiot as to fall for the blatant
manipulation as she scurried down to the kitchen. He'd
clearly got something important on tomorrow that
he'd travelled halfway across the world to deal with, and
he'd called round to see her on the off chance rather than
spend the evening alone.

But he *had* called round, and to her. Not some model
type or one of the many numbers in the little black book
she was sure he'd got.

She savoured the thought for a moment as she whisked
the sticks of spaghetti out of their long tube on the top of
the breakfast bar, and then as she put the lid back on the
glass tube she realised what she was doing. Dangerous,
dangerous, dangerous, she told herself sternly. Okay, a
good few years had passed since that night she had run
away from him with shame and hurt tearing her apart. It
would be good to be able to finally lay the ghost of that
whole episode once and for all, something she'd realised
in the last weeks she had never done. She didn't want to
hate Clay Lincoln; she didn't want to hate anyone.

But—and the but was *huge*—there was a great big difference between letting go of something that was ulti-
mately harming only herself and actually striking up a
relationship, however tenuous, with him. That would
verge on the insane.

He would eat her up and spit her out and not even
notice that he'd done so. That was the sort of man he was;
he lived his life in the fast lane. He had been fascinating
and captivating and a million miles out of her league when

she was sixteen, and nothing had changed. Except…she now had the sense to see the situation clearly.

Her mouth set in a grim line and she opened the fridge, taking out a half-full bottle of white wine and pouring herself a generous glass before she carried on with the meal. Dutch courage maybe, but she needed all the help she could get with Clay upstairs.

'That was wonderful.' As Clay stretched back in his chair Robyn forced herself not to react as hard male muscles bunched and then relaxed again. The broad chest and wide, very male shoulders were shown off to perfection by the thin, lightweight shirt he was wearing. By the time she had trotted upstairs from the kitchen earlier with two steaming plates of spaghetti Bolognese, he had discarded the tie he'd been wearing and had undone the first few buttons of his shirt. It had caused an immediate rush of blistering awareness she could have done without.

'I'm glad you enjoyed it.' Robyn smiled brightly, determined not to dwell on what seeing him at her table did to her fragile equilibrium. 'There's apple and almond pie for dessert, or chocolate mousse? Both shop bought I'm afraid.'

'There's not any custard to go with the pie, is there?' Clay asked hopefully.

Robyn swallowed. The slight touch of boyishness was dynamite. 'Sure,' she said evenly. 'I can make you some.'

'Great. Pie then, please.' He stood up as he spoke and reached across for her plate which he piled on top of his own.

'What are you doing?' she asked quickly.

'I'll wash the dishes while you get the pie,' he said offhandedly, as though the two of them squeezed into the limited confines of the kitchen was nothing at all to worry about. Which it probably wasn't for him, Robyn reflected silently.

'Don't be silly, you're the guest.' She rose herself, reaching across for the plates, and then paused as he surveyed her with cool ice-blue eyes. 'May I?' She indicated to the plates with a brittle smile, determined not to be intimidated by his piercing perusal.

'No, Robyn, you may not,' he countered easily, before turning and making his way to the stairs.

Impossible, infuriating, *arrogant* man. Robyn stood for a moment more, her face mutinous, and then followed him down to the kitchen where, to her dismay, she saw him with his sleeves rolled up and his hands deep in soapy water. She stared at him, her whole stomach somersaulting. This was getting far too cosy and, worse, the touch of domesticity only served to heighten and accentuate the dark maleness at the heart of his attraction.

He turned to look at her, his expression mildly exasperated. 'Stop frowning.' And he turned back to the dishes.

'I'm not.' She knew she had been. 'It's just that I prefer to be in charge in my own kitchen.'

'You cooked the meal; you're getting the pie; you are in charge for crying out loud,' he said irritably, his tone making it quite clear he considered this a pathetic conversation.

Short of wrestling him out of the place—which wasn't an option—she had no choice but to accept defeat gracefully, Robyn conceded reluctantly, because this *was* a pathetic conversation! 'Do you want coffee?' she snapped abruptly.

'Please. Black.' He patently ignored her tone.

Once the custard was ready Robyn cut two pieces of pie and popped them into the microwave, just as the coffee machine began its chugging. Clay had wandered across to stand at the side of her, and now he gave the custard an idle stir in its bowl before surreptitiously bringing the spoon to his mouth.

'Hey! I saw that.' She was half laughing at the childish action as she turned to face him, and he grinned back at her, the laughter lines radiating from his eyes. And then, like the time in the car, their glances held and lengthened.

Robyn was aware of the ping of the microwave but for the life of her she couldn't respond to it. One strong hand tilted her chin as the brilliant gaze continued to hold her fast, and then he pulled her closer to him, her figure slight against the height and breadth of his.

Slowly the black head bent and Robyn made no effort to try to evade his lips. Rhyme and reason had gone out of the window, her body was dictating events now. Languorously her head with its mass of high-bobbing curls fell back against the muscled curve of his arm, and his mouth was hard and urgent on hers.

She made a little sound deep in her throat and he answered it with one of his own, his hands moving down to shape her softness into his hard frame as her arms wound round his neck.

The kiss was almost savage in its intensity but Robyn's mouth was as hungry as his, the frantic pulse beating at the base of her slender throat echoing the hard slam of Clay's heart against his ribcage.

She was arched back, his body bent over hers, and his lips trailed over her throat and into the soft swell of her breasts before moving back to her mouth with renewed fire. She was taking in the wildly intoxicating scent of him and she could feel the blood singing through her veins, feel each separate pulse throb.

She had known it would be like this. As they continued

to devour each other she was aware she was meeting him passion for passion but she felt no timidity, just a desperate need to get closer still. His hands were roaming over her body, moulding her into him and seemingly possessed of a feverish need to know every inch of her, and as his fingers caressed her breasts through the material of the vest top she was aware of their peaks hard and aching beneath his flesh.

'You're so fresh, so beautiful…' His voice was thick and throaty against her mouth. 'I've wanted to do this from the moment I saw you again.'

She had wanted it too. Through the throbbing desire she was aware of her mind warning her about something, something important, but his hands and mouth were the only things that were real. She was melting, dissolving into him, and she couldn't think.

When a phone began to ring somewhere it didn't register on Robyn's whirling senses until she felt Clay stiffen. He pulled her closer for a moment, as though in protest, but the sound went on and on and Robyn realised the ring wasn't her phone.

'My mobile.' His lips had eased to a gentle caress and he gave her one last kiss before straightening and letting her go. 'I'm waiting for a call from the States; I'd better take it.'

A call from the States? He could have been talking in double Dutch so completely was she unable to take it in.

She leant back against the kitchen cupboards and watched him leave the room, her head spinning and her knees weak with the force of the physical storm that had exploded within her.

His footsteps on the stairs informed her he was going to the sitting room where he had left his jacket, but it was a full minute before she could move, and then it was to only sink onto one of the stools under the small breakfast bar.

Had she completely lost her mind? She placed her hand on her heart which was pounding so hard it actually hurt. What had she been thinking of? She gave a little whimper and then froze at the sound. This was Clay Lincoln. *Clay Lincoln.* She shook her head and then reached blindly for the coffee pot, pouring herself a cup with shaking hands and drinking it straight down, black and scalding hot. It helped, a little.

'It's all right, it's all right.' She whispered the words to herself, walking over to the sink and wetting a piece of kitchen roll with cold water before dabbing her hot cheeks. It wasn't as though they had ended up in bed or anything. Her heart gave an enormous jerk at the thought.

She had been crazy for a few moments, that was all, but it was the fault of the blistering sexual awareness Clay always evoked in her with so little effort. He was the one man, the only man who turned her emotions upside down and inside out so she didn't know what she was doing.

Her insides tightened. And now she had to face him again. She swayed backwards and forwards for a moment before she realised what she was doing and stopped abruptly. For goodness' sake, girl, pull yourself together, she told herself caustically. She was *not* going to crumple in front of him, not Clay.

She would prepare a tray with the desserts and coffee, and take it upstairs as though nothing had happened down here. Because it hadn't, not really. The lie didn't help at all. Okay, so *something* had happened, but only to her. To a man like Clay a few passionate kisses were nothing.

If he mentioned it, and she prayed he wouldn't, she'd laugh lightly and make a little offhand comment, blaming her response on the wine. Easy and relaxed and faintly amused, that was the way she'd play it. Then she'd make it plain she had work to do, and exit Clay with the minimum of embarrassment all round.

By the time she had busied herself fixing the tray her cheeks had lost their fiery colour, and as she climbed the stairs to the sitting room it was just in time to hear Clay say, his voice warm, 'Okay, Margo, I'll see you tomorrow when I land. And book a table at Syke's; you deserve a bit of pampering for being such an angel.'

Margo? And dinner at some special place or other? *Pampering?* Robyn tried, she *really* tried not to let the rage show as she swept into the room, her voice high as she said gaily, 'Dessert's now served, and then I really must get down to some work, Clay. I don't like to be rude but I'm going to have to throw you out once you've eaten.'

'That was a business associate in the States.' Clay had turned to face her, his expression unreadable as he took in Robyn's brittle, fixed smile and the angry colour staining her cheeks bright pink. 'Margo Bower.'

'Oh, yes?' Her tone indicated she couldn't care less who it was, it was no business of hers. 'Help yourself to the custard, won't you?'

'She also happens to be my father's youngest sister.'

Robyn had been occupied in whisking the contents of the tray onto the table, and her hands froze for just the merest of moments before she said, 'Your aunt?' Was he lying? But then, why would he bother? And he'd come up with something better!

'My aunt,' he confirmed evenly. 'She's been holding the fort this weekend and something's blown up today that will need sorting tomorrow morning. As I won't be back in time we've just gone through what needs to be done.' And then, Clay being Clay, he added, 'You thought it was a girlfriend of mine, didn't you?' still in the low even tone.

Robyn stopped fiddling with the coffee cups and raised her head slowly. Okay, so he wanted to call a spade a spade—fine. This was her chance to make it clear exactly how she felt.

'I thought it was a possibility,' she said quietly, 'and there would be nothing wrong with that, Clay. You are a free agent, after all. And there's absolutely nothing between us.'

'I disagree.' He moved over to the table and she forced herself to stand perfectly still. 'And while we're on the subject, if I was involved with someone I wouldn't have kissed you like that a few minutes ago. That isn't my style. I believe in fidelity for as long as a relationship lasts.'

She nodded, keeping her back very stiff and her chin high. 'But as there *is* nothing between us it's all relative anyway.'

He stared at her for a moment more and then relaxed, a visible decision. He sat down at the table and reached for his pie, pouring a liberal amount of custard on top of the steaming pastry and then beginning to eat with every appearance of enjoyment. Robyn could do nothing else but follow suit, although every muscle in her body was rigid with tension.

She forced the pie down, almost choking on every mouthful and trying desperately to appear as cool and controlled as Clay was.

'Coffee?' Clay had reached for the coffee jug and poured himself a cup, and now his hand hovered over her cup.

'Thank you.' She managed a nod and a smile and hoped her face hadn't cracked like it felt it had.

She was sipping the hot liquid and praying this terrible evening would soon be over when Clay said, his tone conversational and pleasant, 'We are going to be lovers, Robyn, so you might as well face the fact.'

The coughing and spluttering that followed caused her eyes to stream, courtesy of the coffee going down the wrong way, and when she had mopped herself up and her voice was her own again, she said, 'You're mad, insane. I have absolutely no intention of going to bed with you so *you* might as well face *that* fact.'

'You want me just as much as I want you,' Clay continued imperturbably, apparently not in the least put out by her declaration. 'And you know it. You dream of me; you burn for me when you are awake and when you are asleep; imagine how it will be between us when we make love. I know this because I feel the same, and I am not a man to live on dreams indefinitely. I want the reality. And what I want, I take.'

What was he saying? She could barely take it in. This wasn't real, it couldn't be. She dredged up anger to combat the panic and—humiliatingly—the thrilling excitement his words had caused. 'You'd like to think that, wouldn't you?' she bit out scathingly. 'But the trouble is, Clay, you've been so used to taking what you want when you want it that you can't understand there might be a woman somewhere who doesn't want to sleep with you. Money can't buy everything you know.'

'Money doesn't come into it,' he said calmly. 'And I am more than willing to admit there must be millions of women who wouldn't want to share my bed. You are not one of them. And don't get me wrong, I'm not saying that I think you like the way you feel. You've made it very clear you would prefer to have nothing to do with me, but physically you know there is something between us that defies logic.'

'Don't tell me what I know!' She was frightened, but of herself, not of him, of what she might reveal to those piercing silver eyes.

'You want me, Robyn, and after one night in my arms it will all seem so simple,' the unrelenting voice continued. 'Whoever this guy was who caused you to so distrust the male sex, forget him. There will be truth between us, honesty at all times, and that way no one will get hurt. We can enjoy each other without professions of undying love and ridiculous promises neither of us can keep.' He had settled back in his chair, perfectly relaxed.

Her mouth had fallen slightly open in her amazement and shock, and now she shut it with a little snap. Play it cool, Robyn, she told herself silently, as the desire to fling the contents of her coffee cup straight into his handsome, self-assured face became almost unbearable. 'I don't sleep around, Clay,' she said coldly. 'I would have hoped you knew that.'

'Neither do I,' he countered swiftly. 'And ditto.'

'And my heart as well as my body would have to be involved in a sexual relationship,' she continued steadily.

'If you don't mind me saying so, that's where you went wrong with this guy who broke your heart. You obviously gave him everything and it wasn't reciprocated. With us we would have loyalty and honesty as the basis of our relationship, and the knowledge that we intend to give each other pleasure and no pain.'

Was he mad or was it her? Because one of them was quite insane! Robyn suddenly had the feeling she was in the middle of a rather bad play. And the final curtain needed to come down now.

'At the moment you don't like me because you feel

threatened by the physical attraction between us,' Clay continued smoothly. 'It makes you feel vulnerable, exposed. When that's dealt with you would find it'd be good between us in all areas, not just in bed. We'd have fun, Robyn. I promise you.'

It was the sensual undertone in the last words that told Robyn she had to end this conversation right now. Or rather her body's reaction to them as a wave of heat flooded through her.

'At the risk of sounding like a heroine from a thirties movie, I'm not that kind of girl,' she said, keeping her voice light and dry with enormous effort. 'The liking and bones of the relationship would have to come first, not after the bed bit.'

He seemed to consider her words for a moment, his head slightly on one side as he stared at her with clear silver-blue eyes in which she could read nothing. 'Okay.' He finished his coffee in one gulp and rose to his feet.

Robyn looked up at him. His voice had been quiet and faintly amused, but she couldn't see what he was really thinking because the barrier of his amazing crystal eyes was firmly in place. 'What do you mean, okay?' she asked suspiciously.

'We'll spend time getting to know each other for a while.'

'I don't want to get to know you, Clay,' she said quickly, her heart jerking and then racing like a greyhound.

'You can't have it both ways, Robyn,' he said in a voice that was patiently reasonable. Overly *insultingly* patiently reasonable. 'If you weren't so scared of getting involved in a physical relationship again—' what did he mean, again? she thought wryly '—I would have bedded you long before this. We both know if I start to make love to you, really start to make love to you, you wouldn't stop me. You wouldn't be able to stop me.'

The arrogance of it caused her to blink even as her innate honesty forced her to admit—silently—that he was absolutely right. It also pointed out one little fact that made it imperative she never slept with Clay. *She loved him.* The knowledge had been there all the time since they'd first met again, and it was that which was scaring her half to death. She wasn't over him; she would never be over Clay Lincoln. She had lied to herself for years. Fought against admitting it even to herself.

'Perhaps, perhaps not,' she countered quietly. 'But I do know if I slept with you as things are now I would hate myself.'

Now it was his turn to blink, and there was a peculiar expression on his face as he said, after a long pause, 'Then, we will have to be patient until you can tell me you wouldn't hate yourself because that would be as unacceptable to me as it is to you.' And he sounded as though he meant it.

'And what if I can never say it?' she said in a little rush, her heart pounding. 'What then?'

'You will, Robyn.' It was quiet but carried a wealth of intent. 'The timing was wrong all those years ago but whatever is between us now was there then, and it hasn't died. If anything it is stronger.'

How right you are, she thought with a terribly irony. But it's love on my side and just physical attraction on yours, and that makes you the most dangerous thing in the world. She'd survived one encounter of being rejected by him; when he tired of her this time—and he would tire of her as he'd already made very clear with his clever words about no ridiculous promises and no lasting commitment—she wouldn't come to the surface again. And she was worth more than that, she told herself bitterly.

But she had whetted his interest the night of Guy's birthday by her coolness, although it hadn't been intentional and she certainly hadn't been playing hard-to-get. He was a tough, cynical, worldly man who was used to women throwing themselves at him, and she had been a little different. That was all it was on his side. Whereas she...

Robyn took a long, deep breath and stood to her feet. If she didn't go along with this façade of 'getting to know each other' he would pursue her relentlessly, he was that type of man. But if, after a few weeks or months he realised she wasn't what he thought she was, he would lose interest, and probably by then there would be some other woman ready to console him. In fact she could guarantee it. They were probably queueing up already.

'Okay, we date for a while.' It took all of her willpower and then some to sound so calm and matter-of-fact. 'When you happen to be in the country of course,' she added with a touch of sarcasm, 'work permitting.'

'Work will permit exactly what I tell it to.' He was walking to the staircase as he spoke and it took her by surprise. Was he going? She hadn't expected him to concur to her demands so easily.

'I flew over from the States to see you today,' he continued without turning round, 'and I shall do it again when necessary.'

'You said—' She had followed him and now stopped speaking abruptly when he swung round at the top of the stairs and faced her. Then she forced herself to go on quickly, 'You said you came back on business.'

'No, Robyn, *you* said I had come back on business,' he said softly. He kissed the top of her nose, a light kiss, even teasing, but it was enough to make her stiffen and tense as the subtle magnetism increased tenfold.

'I might not have been here,' she said feverishly, taking an involuntary step backwards away from him. 'I do go out you know.'

'Then I would have been disappointed,' he said coolly. 'Goodnight, Robyn. I'll see myself out.'

She was too taken aback and confused to do anything other than watch him descend, and when the sound of the front door shutting a few moments later brought her out of the trance she'd fallen into, her legs gave way and she sank down onto the top step, her head whirling. She felt as though she'd been bulldozed!

How was it that she was doing exactly what she had promised herself she would never do, and getting involved with Clay? she asked herself bewilderly. How had he *managed* that?

And the answer came back, uncompromising and frightening. Because he was astute enough, intuitive enough, to sense he had her in the palm of his hand. But— and this was the only thing that helped the hot panic that was in danger of taking her over to subside a little—he thought it was mere sexual desire that was attracting her. He didn't know she loved him.

And whatever it took, *whatever* it took, he never would know. It would be the final humiliation.

CHAPTER SIX

ROBYN threw herself into work for the rest of the evening and by the time she fell into bed the midnight oil had well and truly burnt out, it being nearly three o'clock. Nevertheless it was a good half an hour before she could persuade her racing mind to let her sleep, and then she was awake again at six with Clay's name on her lips after a particularly erotic dream that left her aroused and aching. And longing, *burning* to see him again.

There was no chance of more sleep, and even after a long, cool shower the sexual arousal had her feeling restless and cross with herself. She couldn't believe that he had swept back into her life after all these years and had just taken over her emotions again. It was—she searched for the words—it was degrading and mortifying and so *unfair*.

Once dressed, she marched up and down the sitting room for a while and then forced herself to go downstairs and make some coffee which she took up onto the tiny balcony. The morning air was warm when she opened the full-length windows—it was going to be another lovely day—but her agitation had her drinking the coffee in little sharp gulps as she scanned the vista beyond without really seeing it, her mind in turmoil.

It would be emotional suicide to agree to Clay's proposition, she knew that, so why did a little voice in the back of her mind keep suggesting that maybe, *maybe*, if she allowed him into her life and her body, he might find he was falling for her too?

112

Clutching at straws. She nodded at the thought. Cass and Guy had let enough little comments drop during the years for her to know that Clay was a dedicated love-'em-and-leave-'em type.

Perhaps he had been so in love with his wife that no one could take her place? She deliberately considered the thought that had tormented her for years, if she was being truthful. Certainly she had to face the fact that he'd forget her as quickly as he could click his fingers once the affair came to an end. And that was all she could hope for with Clay, an affair. He would leave her with no pride, no self-respect; everything she had worked for over the last years would be as ashes. And that mustn't happen.

She finished the coffee and padded back down to the kitchen whereupon she forced herself to eat a bowl of cereal and two slices of toast. At eight o'clock she was seated at her desk in the office, and when Drew arrived Robyn was bright and breezy and very businesslike.

At half-past nine the telephone rang, and whether it was sixth sense or women's intuition she didn't know, but Robyn told Drew to leave it and let the answer machine take the call.

'Robyn...' The deep, husky voice brought the blood rushing to her face and made her toes curl under the desk. 'Just a quick call to say how much I enjoyed the meal last night and the company even more. I'm leaving for the States in a few minutes but I'll be back at the weekend. Save Saturday for me?' There was a slight pause. 'And take care.'

There was a full thirty seconds of silence before Drew said, her tone one of awe, 'Wow! What a way to start the day!'

Robyn hoped her cheeks weren't as visibly hot as they felt. She stared at Drew, and then said, 'That was—'

'I know who it was.' Drew sighed enviously. 'There's only one man I've met recently who has a voice like that. He's *gorgeous*, Robyn. Utterly drop-dead gorgeous.'

'It's not what you think,' Robyn said hastily. 'Really.'

'No?' Drew opened her baby-blue eyes wider and gave a Marilyn Monroe pout. 'Then, make it what I'm thinking, Robyn. This is one hunk you just can't let escape. They don't come gift-wrapped like him but once in a lifetime.'

It was a toss up who was surprised more when Robyn burst into tears in the next moment, but the maternal side of Drew came immediately to the fore and Robyn was bustled upstairs for tea and chocolate biscuits—Drew's answer to all of life's emergencies. Especially the two-legged kind.

Quite how she came to be telling Drew the whole story, Robyn didn't know, but over the next ten minutes it all spilled out; from the time she was twelve years old and captivated by a dark, sleek Adonis, to the present day. Even the episode when she was sixteen didn't seem so hard to talk about with Drew's arm about her shoulders and her sympathy flowing in waves.

'I knew there was someone.' Drew gave her a big hug when she finished talking, passing her another tissue as she did so.

'How?' Robyn sniffed mournfully. 'How did you know?'

'Because when a woman looks like you do and gives the brush off to every man in sight, it has to mean some-one in the past has done a good job on her heart,' Drew said with all the wisdom of her twenty-eight years. 'And he did, didn't he?'

'It…it was my fault.' She didn't know why she had to defend Clay but somehow she did. 'I threw myself at him.'

'Oh, come on, Robyn.' Drew was scathing. 'You were sweet sixteen and never been kissed, and he was twenty-three and pretty experienced, I bet. He was a rat!'

She didn't want Drew to hate Clay, but it did feel good to have someone so totally on her side. Robyn found she felt a bit better.

'Why didn't you say anything before?' Drew asked with a touch of amazement. 'We've been friends for ever.' And then she answered herself immediately with, 'But you aren't like me, are you? You've always been a deep one, Robyn, and never one to wear your heart on your sleeve.'

'Oh, Drew.' Robyn stared at the other girl forlornly.

'Which means you're playing with fire now.' Drew looked at her unhappily. 'I think I better make another cup of tea.'

They didn't get much work done that morning but Robyn found that by telling someone the whole miserable story a great weight had lifted off her heart. It hadn't changed her predicament, but in admitting her true feelings for Clay out loud to another human being some of the shame and humiliation of the past was gone. This was life—not always nice and certainly not always fair or tidy, but she was one of millions of mortals who made mistakes and loved where they should not.

As Drew had said, and with deep feeling, 'Welcome to the human race, kiddo.'

Surprisingly that night Robyn slept like a baby and awoke on Tuesday morning feeling positive. She could handle this, *she could*. And once Clay realised that anything of a sexual nature was a no-go, he might even start to look at her as a friend. She *was* Cass's sister after all so it was likely their paths might cross now and again.

She ignored the very pertinent fact that their paths hadn't crossed in years, and also the stab in her heart at the thought of being on the perimeter of Clay's life and hearing about—even maybe watching—his affairs with other women, and concentrated fiercely on work. She knew where she was with that.

By Friday evening Robyn was telling herself she had to psych herself up carefully for the following day. Clay hadn't contacted her personally although mid-week a huge bunch of hot-house orchids had been delivered to the house, with a little note which had said, 'Looking forward to Saturday, C.' Drew had looked at the flowers and had exhaled long and loud.

'They must have cost a small fortune, Robyn.'

'At the risk of sounding cynical, he can afford the grand gestures, Drew,' Robyn had said sadly.

'Maybe.' Drew had continued to look goggle-eyed at the magnificent plumes. 'But considering the most my ex's have trumped up is a bunch of off-the-peg chrysan-themums or freesias, he's got style.'

'I *like* freesias.'

'Oh, Robyn!'

Drew left at just after half-past five and Robyn contin-ued working at her desk until six, at which point she gazed at the piles of paperwork awaiting her attention and sighed. She had interviewed three prospective employees during the week and she and Drew had decided on the last one, an extremely capable, plump, bustling redhead who was thirty-three years old and had taken a few years out to be at home whilst her two children were tiny. Now the second child had started full-time nursery Fiona had decided she wanted to get back into the world of the big kids—as she'd put it. She was a little loud, a flamboyant dresser and her sense of humour had been infectious, and Robyn and Drew had felt she'd fit in very nicely.

However, due to a trip she and her husband had arranged to France she was unable to take up employment for another three weeks, so until then the mountain of paperwork and hectic, non-stop schedule wasn't going to get any better.

She would be working half the night again. Robyn sighed once more and had just reached for one of the files when a knock at the front door brought her to her feet.

'Clay!' As she opened the front door her heart jolted up into her throat and almost stopped. She hadn't expected this; he was supposed to be back in England tomorrow.

He was wearing black jeans and a black denim shirt—more like the young, university Clay than the immaculately designer-suited present-day one—and he took her breath away.

'Hi.' It was easy and relaxed and he smiled slowly, the devastating smile that always had the power to send her senses into hyperdrive, the silver eyes softening and crinkling at the corners.

'This isn't Saturday,' she said stupidly.

'No, it isn't,' he agreed softly, stepping forward and taking her in his arms. 'It's Friday, the most incredible, fantastic Friday ever.' And he kissed her, long and hard right there on the doorstep. 'Because,' he added as he raised his mouth from hers, 'I'm holding you, feeling you, tasting you.'

'Clay, you should have phoned.' She wriggled loose.

'Have you missed me, Robyn?' He stepped over the threshold into the house and she stared at his broad back for a moment before she shut the front door. Typical, she thought bewilderly. Not a thought in his head that she might be doing something else tonight, seeing someone else.

And then she had to rethink that thought when he swung round and said quietly, 'Are you free tonight, Robyn?'

She stared at him, aware that that one kiss had brought her body alive in a way that was positively lascivious, and that despite every warning she had given herself over and over and over the last few days she was madly, wildly happy to see him.

'Too late.' His hands went round her slim waist and he was looking down into the velvet brown of her eyes as he said, a touch drily, 'You hesitated a mite too long, sweetheart.'

'I'm not really free,' she objected quickly, the knowledge that he was railroading her again strong. 'I've masses of work to do, some of it urgent.'

'Sorry, as an excuse that one is just not good enough.'

'It's the truth!' she protested indignantly.

'I don't doubt it,' he murmured, kissing her again until she was gasping for breath. 'But I'm not playing second fiddle to that—' he indicated her paper-strewn desk with a wave of his hand '—or anything else,' he added softly.

Her skin was hot, *she* was hot, deep inside in the core of her, and she was aware Clay knew exactly how his body was affecting her. It was there in the slight tilt to his hard firm mouth and the silver glint in his eyes.

'What did you have in mind?' she asked distractedly, and then blushed furiously when she read the wry expression on his handsome face. 'I mean—'

'I know what you meant, Robyn,' he said soothingly, and she wondered why one man—this man—had been given so much of absolutely everything that made a male a male. 'Dinner at my place?' he suggested evenly 'A thank you for the meal you rustled up for me at such short notice on Sunday.'

'Your place?' Alarm bells were ringing furiously. 'I don't think so.' Talk about walking into the lion's den!

'Don't you trust me?' he asked sadly.

She looked him full in the face. 'Not an inch.'

He grinned, his eyes stroking over her face. Unexpectedly his hand lifted and tilted her chin. 'Wise girl.' He let her go in the next moment and ridiculously she felt bereft. 'But in this instance you'll be quite safe, my houseckeeper will be around. Added to which—' and now the piercing eyes became deadly serious '—you aren't ready for me yet.'

Her heart was fluttering against her ribs like a captive bird at the look on his face, and in that moment all she wanted to do was to move into his arms again, to nestle close and slide her hands down the muscled column of his neck and inside his half-opened shirt. She wanted to feel his skin, tangle her fingers in the dark silky warmth of the body hair just visible in the V of the denim shirt, explore the hard, male chest.

She stepped back a pace sharply, wondering how she could ever have been so stupid as to think she was over Clay Lincoln. She had loved him all her life; she would die loving him. 'I'll have to change but it won't take a minute.'

'Fine.' He walked over to the windows at the end of the room which looked out onto the paved garden. 'I'll wait here.'

Robyn took her cue from the way Clay was dressed and changed quickly into casual cream drawstring trousers and a short-sleeved, waist-length cotton top in pastel blue. She combed out her hair from the high knot on top of her head it had been in all day, and then hesitated as her hands went to draw it up again. Her scalp was aching slightly and she balked at the idea of further pressure. She'd leave it loose.

She was back downstairs again in under five minutes, and Clay was still standing where she'd left him looking out of the windows. He turned to face her as she reached the bottom step, his eyes flashing over her, their silver light very bright. 'You look sixteen again with your hair like that,' he said quietly, his face unreadable.

It startled her. He hadn't made any reference to the past other than in a derogatory nature, and she found it acutely painful to be reminded that he'd thought she was a flirtatious little coquette then, a provocative tease who had been trying out her new-found femininity on any male within kissing distance.

She smiled stiffly. 'Gallons of water have passed under the bridge since those days,' she said tightly. He probably thought deep inside that if her behaviour with him on the night of Cass's wedding was anything to go by she had got exactly what she'd asked for with this mysterious man from university, who according to her sister had broken her heart.

'That's for sure.' For a second his eyes were as hard and clear and uncompromising as diamonds, a ruthless quality to his mouth that hadn't been there a moment before. And then it was gone and he was walking towards her, smiling easily.

Robyn responded in a like manner, making small talk as they left the house and walked out to the car, but inside she was trembling slightly. What had happened, what had he been remembering to put that expression in his eyes? she asked herself silently. He *was* different to the Clay of old, but just how different she hadn't realised until this very moment.

By the time they drove into Windsor the air was heavy with the lazy golden twilight that seemed to last endlessly in the summer. Shafts of sun were slanting through the trees of the road they were following, and then Clay drew up outside large wrought-iron gates set in an eight-feet-high stone wall which he opened automatically from the car window.

Once inside the wide drive was flanked by towering oaks, but within moments they emerged into a wide semi-circle leading to a beautiful, stone-built Victorian house surrounded on three sides by massive cypresses.

'It's wonderful, Clay.' They had said very little on the drive to the house, but now Robyn turned to the big dark figure at the side of her, her voice warm. 'What a gorgeous place to live.' Gorgeous? It was like a mini paradise all of its own.

He watched her face for a moment and then he smiled slowly. 'I bought it some years ago from a friend of a friend who was emigrating to Canada,' he said quietly. 'It'd been in his family from when it was built in 1870, and from the first moment I stepped in the door I knew I had to have it. It felt good, solid. Life has been happy within its walls, you can feel it.'

She stared at him, absolutely amazed by his sensitivity, and then flushed hotly when he said, his tone sardonic, 'Surprised I've got a soul, Robyn?'

'Not at all,' she lied swiftly. 'Don't be silly.'

He continued to survey her for a moment more before cutting the engine, and then he said, his voice very even and cool, 'I had a privileged upbringing by most standards. My mother was English and my father American, and both families were well-off, my father's particularly so, but my maternal grandparents' farm in Sussex was a haven for two small inquisitive boys with acres to roam about in. That was fortunate as we were often dumped there while my parents sorted out yet another quarrel.'

'I'm sorry.' She didn't know what else to say.

He was looking through the windscreen now, his profile hard, as he continued, 'The trouble was my mother's inability to be faithful. She had scores of lovers by all accounts, but my father—who was twenty years older than her—loved her and turned a blind eye where he could. Unfortunately my mother sometimes made that impossible, and then we'd be shipped off to our grandparents from wherever we were in the world. Every time they resolved their differences we seemed to move to a new home, a new start—' his voice was very cynical '—so Mitch and I never seemed able to make permanent friends or put down roots.'

'Did...did you live in America?' she asked softly, aware that it was anathema to him to talk like this, to reveal anything of himself.

'All over the place,' he answered shortly. 'My father's shipping empire, which he'd inherited from his father, made it possible for any location in the world to be within their price range. We hated it, Mitch and I. The only time we were happy was when we were on the farm in Sussex. That's why I was determined to come to university in England, to be near my grandparents.'

'And they had the potting shed?' she asked lightly, aiming to bring him out of the past.

'What?' For a moment his face was blank, and then the darkness that had gripped it lifted and he smiled, nodding as he said, 'Oh, yes, the potting shed. We had our first drink, our first stolen cigarette in its hallowed walls, watched only by the family of mice who lived there.'

He was opening his car door as he spoke; clearly the glimpse into his past had finished, Robyn acknowledged silently. But that was fine. Although she was burning with curiosity, another part of her brain was warning her very strongly that everything she learnt about him, every personal little detail, wasn't going to make it any easier when this tenuous relationship finished. And it would finish. She would have known that even if he hadn't spelled it out for her.

From the outside the house had appeared large but not excessively so; however once Clay opened the front door and Robyn stepped into the hall she realised the building was huge, even before Clay told her there were eight bedrooms all with *ensuite*.

The hall was vast and the staircase a thing of beauty all on its own, being of ornate iron drag-painted in gold, but Robyn had little time to take in the lush russet carpet and fine paintings on the walls before Clay was introducing her to his housekeeper. Mrs Jones was a tall, slim, attractive woman with a Welsh lilt to her voice who apparently lived with her husband—an invalid—in a bungalow annexe at the back of the house, and Robyn liked her on sight. She was friendly and warm but not gushing.

'Come and have a quick look round and then we'll have a drink before dinner,' Clay said casually, as though he brought women into his house every day of the week. Which he probably did, Robyn reminded herself painfully.

He showed her the upstairs first which seemed to stretch for ever in pale cream carpets, bedroom after bedroom in different colour schemes of peach, lemon, strawberry and other soft shades, until they came to the master bedroom which was uncompromisingly Clay. Maple wood floor, a predominantly stark colour scheme of silver and black, and a huge four-poster bed was *so* him, Robyn thought tensely, as she gingerly poked her head round the door, refusing his invitation to proceed further into the room.

Silken curtains hung at the full length windows which were wide open and led onto a large stone balcony, and the enormous bed was draped with silk sheets and billowy pillows and cushions in abundance.

It was as different to the other rooms as chalk to cheese, and relentlessly masculine. Luxurious, but with a sensuality that was both spartan and hedonistic.

How many women had lounged on those wicked silken sheets and pillows? Robyn thought miserably, replete and satisfied after a long night of lovemaking. They would be glowing, purring like sleek, contented cats and—

'Robyn?'

'What?' She blinked, realising Clay had been talking and she hadn't heard a word.

'I'll show you downstairs and then we can have that drink,' he repeated patiently, 'if you're ready?'

Ready? She didn't know what she was! A candidate for the funny farm at this rate. Certainly she knew that her dreams would have an extra dimension now this room was in her subconscious.

Once downstairs she admired the long light kitchen, the breakfast room, Clay's study, the dining room and the sitting room, and then they were in the high-vaulted drawing room which managed to be grandly impressive yet warm and welcoming at the same time.

Glass doors at the far end of the room led out onto a charming patio which afforded a view of the magnificent grounds, and it was on the table out here that Mrs Jones had placed an ice bucket complete with a bottle of champagne and two big fluted glasses. Robyn suddenly felt deliciously spoilt.

Clay poured them both a glass of the frothy, sparkling wine, his voice very deep and low as he said, 'To us, to getting to know each other a little...better.'

'Is this the line you use with all your women in the beginning?' Robyn asked with a careful lack of expression.

'What?' The glass froze before it reached his lips.

She'd surprised him, annoyed him certainly, and it felt good considering he was tying her up in knots. 'I said—'

'I heard what you said,' he ground out tightly.

Oh, yes, he *definitely* hadn't appreciated that one. 'I just wondered,' she said sweetly. 'You didn't mind me asking, did you?'

'Oh, no, it adds wonderfully to the moment,' he said sarcastically.

She surveyed him steadily. Okay, so she loved him, undeserving rat that he was—Drew's expression, not hers—but that didn't mean she had to act like some dumb bimbo who wasn't aware of his tactics, for goodness' sake. She did have a brain as well as a body. 'So, do you?' She dared to persist.

He stared at her and she looked back at him, keeping her expression sweet and innocent by sheer will-power. He clearly couldn't decide if she was being purposefully facetious or simply ingenuous, but she rather thought he had decided on the former when he said grimly, 'I like to think I have never used a line, as you term it, in my life, Robyn.'

No, you probably didn't have to, she thought waspishly. You just click your fingers and they queue up for the privilege.

'No?' She managed to inject surprise into her voice.

The silver gaze narrowed. 'You seem to have the impression I conduct my love life like a stud horse,' he said evenly.

'Not at all.' She rather wished she hadn't started this

now. She didn't want to hear about his ex's, added to which she had been foolish to think she could provoke him and get away with it.

'I can actually use restraint and finesse when it pleases me to do so,' he said silkily, taking a sip of his champagne as he continued to survey her with the icy-blue gaze.

'I'm sure you can.' She watched him place his glass on the table with wary eyes.

'Let me give you a little demonstration.' The glass was whisked from her already nerveless fingers as he spoke and then she was in his arms and his mouth and tongue were teasing her lips, pleasuring her slowly, subtly but with relentless intent.

He didn't grope or rush her, his lips first toying with hers, then searching her mouth urgently before returning to their teasing. His hands were mounting an easy caress on her skin, first on the bare skin of her arms and then sliding to the silky smooth flesh beneath her top just above her trousers, until her muscles had become fluid and loose.

The pleasure that was mounting was strong and sweet and powerful, a tide of heat that was rising and falling but steadily gathering steam, and she could feel herself quivering in spite of all her efforts to disguise it.

His mouth moved to play with her ears, her throat, one hand brushing the tips of her breasts with a feather-light caress that nevertheless made her moan helplessly.

She was kissing him back wildly now, searching for his mouth, straining against him as she felt his thighs hard against hers, the soft pads of his fingertips rubbing the peaks of her swollen breasts erotically through the thin top.

They had moved—somehow they must have moved although Robyn hadn't been aware of it through her whirling senses—because now she was pressed against the wall of the house, Clay holding her there with his body while his hands and mouth continued the intoxicating, sensual and inexorable assault.

She could feel the intimacy of his arousal and it fired the intensity of her own desire even more, her mind and emotions utterly bemused and captivated.

And then he let her go, stepping back a pace as he left her leaning against the wall. 'You see?' It was cool and controlled, and if she hadn't felt his body's betrayal she would have thought he was totally unmoved. 'Restraint and finesse.'

She was trembling, her heart pounding far too fast, but somewhere in the core of her she found the strength to drum up enough poise to say tightly, 'I don't appreciate a demonstration such as that to make a point, Clay. Please don't think you can repeat it.'

She saw the flash of admiration in his eyes before he could conceal it, and then his expression was hidden from her as he walked across to the table, retrieving both their glasses and turning and handing her hers before he said, 'It wasn't altogether a demonstration, Robyn. I need a little taste of what is to come now and again if I'm going to keep my sanity, because at the moment I'm eating, sleeping, *breathing* you and it's driving me mad.'

'I haven't promised you anything.' Her voice was jerky but the unexpected confession had unnerved her like nothing else could have done.

'I know that, my sweet little brown-eyed temptress,' he murmured softly. 'But you don't have to, not with your mouth. Your body says everything I need to know.'

'How convenient for you,' she said icily, and then glared at him when he laughed quietly.

'You're a formidable opponent, Robyn Brett.'

Opponent? Ridiculously it hurt. This was just a game

to him, she thought painfully. The thrill of the chase and all that. Since she had met him again she had been the very antithesis of the young, starry-eyed teenager who had hung on his every word and had gazed at him adoringly, and it had probably pricked his male ego. Oh, she hated him. And loved him. And if there was anyone who was being driven mad...

'A new toast.' He was looking at her intently and now she stared at him, waiting warily for what was to come. 'To you, my brown-eyed temptress, with your hair of russet-red and your skin of thick warm cream. One day I shall make love to you like you ought to be made love to, but until then I will worship from afar.' He grinned at her, and in spite of herself Robyn couldn't help but smile back. 'With the odd fall from grace now and again,' he added silkily, just as Mrs Jones called them in to dinner.

It was an enchanted evening. Robyn didn't want to enjoy herself, in fact she would have given the world to find out that Clay had grown boring or offensive or tedious over the years, but he was...perfect. Just perfect, she acknowledged silently.

Once they were seated at the splendid dining table with course after course being presented by the reputable Mrs Jones, who turned out to be a magnificent cook, Clay was the epitome of the faultless host. He was charming and funny, the magnetism that was at the root of his dark attraction non-threatening for once. And she found herself laughing and relaxing in a way she could never have imagined even just hours before.

Afterwards Robyn could remember little of what they had talked about, she just knew she had never laughed so much or felt so gloriously vibrantly alive.

They had coffee in the sitting room next to the drawing room, which was smaller and cosier but again had windows opening onto the gardens, and with just a table lamp mellowing the scented darkness from the roses outside the window the effect was magical. And intimate. Robyn was very aware of the intimate, waiting all night long for Clay to make a move.

But at just gone midnight the taxi he had ordered to take her home arrived—Clay having drunk several glasses of champagne, and brandy with his coffee—and they both left the house without so much as a kiss being exchanged. He came with her in the taxi and again she felt she was on tenterhooks, but he merely chatted easily about this and that, his arm round her shoulders and his big body hard against her thigh. And once they arrived in Kensington he walked her to the door while the taxi waited.

'Tomorrow. A drive into the country and dinner at a little place I know, okay?' He tilted her chin up and kissed her lightly. 'I'll pick you up about three in the afternoon, and then you can work in the morning. I presume you want to work?' he added wryly.

'Yes, but I ought to work all day,' she began worriedly, only for him to shake his head as he put a finger to her lips.

'Three is as far as I'll compromise,' he said softly. And then he kissed her again, a quick kiss on her parted lips, and strode back to the taxi.

It waited while she opened the door and put the lights on, and then the engine revved and the car disappeared into the night.

Robyn stood at the window staring out into the dark street for some moments before she went upstairs, and her mind replayed the evening over and over while she had a bath and got ready for bed, her whole being still gloriously tinglingly alive.

This whole relationship was impossible and undeniably dangerous, and she was getting in deeper and deeper every time she saw him. The warning was suddenly impossible to ignore.

She frowned to herself as she pulled out the bed-settee and fetched her duvet and pillows from the big pine chest at the far end of the room, and once settled under the covers tossed and turned for some time as sleep eluded her.

She should never have agreed to his putting up the capital and becoming part of her business for a start; that had been her first mistake. Clay Lincoln as a sleeping partner had not been one of her better decisions. Sleeping partner... She bit her lip hard and after a few more minutes padded down to the kitchen for a mug of cocoa and the obligatory chocolate biscuits.

But he *was* her sleeping partner—in business—and that was how it was going to stay, she affirmed silently, once she was back in bed. She just had to be sensible and on her guard the next little while until he accepted she wasn't in the market for a casual affair. And then, then he would be off. She couldn't hope for anything more, not with Clay.

She repeated the thought again, and then again, ignoring the sick feeling it produced that even the chocolate biscuits couldn't remedy. He didn't want permanency in his private life—his choice. He'd made it clear from the word go. And the trouble was anything less wasn't viable, the way she felt about him. So, stalemate.

She snuggled down under the covers again after finishing the cocoa and biscuits, shutting her eyes, and despite the fact that she had expected to lie awake for hours was asleep in seconds.

CHAPTER SEVEN

THAT summer was the most breathtakingly wonderful on the one hand, and the most excruciatingly miserable on the other, of Robyn's entire life.

After the business in the States was settled which Clay had been involved in at the start of their relationship, he spent four weeks on the trot in England, and they saw each other almost every evening. Robyn soon found that it was useless to say no to a date with Clay; he would simply sweep in, all guns firing, and whisk her away ignoring all her protests as though he was deaf.

Not that she wanted to say no if she was being truthful, which confirmed to her absolutely that no *should* be her answer! Everything they did together was heightened by Clay's fierce zest for living; he could turn the most mundane activities into enchanting times and he did it with a natural expertise that was scary. Because—and Robyn had to keep reminding herself of this a hundred times a day— this affair that wasn't an affair couldn't last. And there the excruciatingly miserable side came to the fore.

Not that he put any pressure on her to take their lovemaking to its logical conclusion. He made it very clear the first week he stayed in England that he expected to kiss and caress her as his right, but that he acknowledged the boundaries she'd put on their physical relationship and was prepared to keep to them...for the present.

And as one summer day made way for another, Robyn found she was discovering more and more about him, about the real man behind the mask Clay adopted to the rest of the world most of the time. Little things, but each one subtly dangerous.

In August he was gone for two weeks again, and to her horror Robyn found she was missing him more than words could express. A small posy of flowers was delivered each day for the whole of the fortnight, and Clay phoned her most evenings. She shivered when she heard his voice, aching for him with a fierce longing that petrified her when she thought about it.

Once he was back in England again they had an evening out with Cass and Guy at Topeka's—Clay's treat—and had a whale of a time, in spite of Cass being as smug as the proverbial cat with the cream.

Robyn tried twice to convince her elder sibling that she and Clay were *not* an item in the way Cass was assuming, but she might as well have saved her breath, she realised at last, admitting defeat. Cass had a distinctly satisfied matchmaking gleam in her eyes and was determined to take credit for finding Robyn the love of her life—which was pretty ironic in the circumstances, Robyn reflected drily.

Nevertheless, Robyn found she couldn't quite bring herself to tell Cass the full facts of her relationship with Clay, which would have put pay to Cass's ideas, and decided she had to let her sister think what she liked in the end. Cass was too close to it all somehow, too linked with Clay, whereas Drew was different. Uncomplicated. And totally on her side.

And after the evening at the nightclub Robyn found she wasn't in a hurry to repeat another foursome with Cass and Guy. She couldn't have explained even to herself how that night had affected her, but being part of two couples had felt so good, so right, so wonderfully *permanent*, that the whole episode had been a bitter-sweet experience which had seen her crying until dawn once she was alone.

Robyn glanced across at Clay now. He was lying next to her on a sunlounger in the grounds of his home, and they were in the shade of a massive weeping-willow tree, the day having been a scorcher. The evening air was thick and sultry, and even the birds seemed exhausted by the heat and unusually silent, only the steady drone of insects coming and going on the following bushes nearby disturbing the summer evening.

'Another glass of wine?' he asked lazily.

He didn't open his eyes as he spoke but somehow she knew he was aware she was looking at him. They had brought a bottle of wine and two glasses down to the little grassy dell beneath the tree some minutes earlier, Mrs Jones having arranged to call them once dinner was ready, and now Robyn took a sip of the rich, fruity red liquid before she said, her voice light, 'No, thanks, I've hardly touched this one.'

The perfume scenting the air from the flowers and bushes was heady, the humid warmth of the evening having brought it out to its fullest and, as Clay opened his eyes and then sat up, his silver eyes scanning her face, Robyn was aware that this was one of those moments she would remember for the rest of her life.

The beautiful garden, the scents in the air, the warmth on her skin and the rich blackcurrant taste of the wine on her tongue, was all a background to the lean dark man at her side. She never looked at him without a thrill flickering down her spine, and tonight, his having picked her up straight from work, he was dressed in beautifully cut trousers and a pale blue silk shirt which was open at the neck and had the sleeves rolled up to reveal strong, muscular arms, his tie and jacket long since discarded. He was magnificent.

'You never truly relax, do you?' It was softy and deep, and more of a statement than a question.

Robyn looked at him, startled. 'Of course I do.' Her response was immediate and defensive. 'That's silly.'

His eyes were narrowed in the pale hazy light, his face still, and then his mouth unexpectedly twisted in a smile that was self-deprecating. 'Not with me,' he qualified quietly. 'And I don't know why. I have done everything you asked, have I not? But I am still the enemy.'

Those silver-blue eyes saw far too much. Robyn stared at him, not sure how to play down the sudden confrontation. 'That's silly too,' she said carefully. 'Of course you aren't an enemy.'

'*The* enemy, Robyn,' he clarified softly. 'As in the male sex. What on earth did this guy do to you to make you so wary? He didn't abuse you? Physically I mean?' he asked grimly.

She was utterly shocked and it showed. 'Of course not!'

'But mentally, emotionally, you have scars,' Clay murmured. 'Maybe sexually too.'

She really didn't know if she could handle this. She sat up with a tenseness that was tangible, her voice very controlled as she said, 'This is crazy, Clay. I don't know what you're thinking but you seem to have let your imagination run away with you.'

'You don't want to want me but you do.' The soft voice was relentless. 'You're as hungry as I am, but you don't trust me, not even now after all these weeks. And I'm not going to take you into my bed until you do. I promised you I wouldn't rush you, that I could wait until you're ready, but even more importantly I promised myself because I know once I really start to make love to you there will be no turning back for either of us. And I want no regrets, Robyn. No lies, no, ''I was swept away by the moment.'' It will be a conscious decision for you, because you need and want me more than anything else and there'll be no self-reproach in the morning.'

The male ego again! The incredible, conquering-hero syndrome. Robyn took a big gulp of wine and swallowed before she said, her voice brittle, 'Don't you ever consider the possibility that one day you might not actually get exactly what you want?'

He smiled again but this time it was merely a twitch of the hard firm lips. 'Where you are concerned?' he asked huskily. 'Never. Because if I did I might forget my promises and take you into my arms and start to ravish you until we go to heaven and back.'

Robyn felt a shuddering excitement even as she warned herself not to betray anything to the metallic eyes that seemed able to cut through all the layers of her defences. 'How do you know we would be sexually compatible?' she said offhandedly, forcing her voice to sound even and unconcerned. 'Lots of people aren't, even if they fancy each other like mad initially.'

'The voice of experience?' He was mocking her now, and even though the teasing was gentle it caught her on the raw.

'Oh, I don't doubt for a minute every woman you've ever wanted has just fallen into your arms,' she said cuttingly, draining the last of her wine. 'One hundred per cent success rate for Clay Lincoln.'

If she had been looking at him, rather than staring angrily into the dusky night, she would have noticed the hard male face had tightened, his mouth straightening, but his voice was very quiet when he said, 'One hundred per cent is a little high for anyone, don't you think?'

'Oh, come on!' She didn't know why she was so rattled. 'Do you mean to tell me there's a woman out there somewhere who's said no?'

'I wasn't aware of telling you anything.'

It was his complete stillness rather than the tone of his voice that brought her eyes flashing back to his face, but what she read there froze any response she might have made. She stared at him, her eyes wide and dark, and wondered who had caused the depth of pain scoring his face. Because it had to be a person, a woman. His wife? He had never talked about losing his wife, but then this hadn't been a conversation about the pain of loss but something quite different. She didn't understand this.

'I'm sorry, Clay.' It was a whisper. 'I wasn't trying to open old wounds.'

She watched him take a long, deep breath and then his voice came more or less evenly when he said, 'I know that.'

They were silent for a moment, Clay turning from her so his face was in profile as he stared across the slumbering garden, and Robyn sitting in numb misery. Some small, buried part of her was saying, Aren't you glad he's suffered a little after what he put you through? Aren't you pleased he hasn't had it all his own way? And she answered the silent voice with all her heart as she realised there was no shred of satisfaction or gratification in her thinking. There was envy, jealousy, even hate, against this unknown woman who had so captured his heart as to make him look like he did now, and that was awful. She acknowledged her weakness even as she knew it was still there.

And then he began to talk, and suddenly Robyn realised she was hearing from the essence of the man. It was there in the bitter, clipped tone of his voice and the almost tangible anger. 'My mother—' He stopped abruptly. 'Well, I've told you a little of what my mother was like,' he continued almost immediately. 'When Mitch and I were eleven she put my father through a particularly humiliating experience by having an affair with one of his close friends. My father worshipped the ground she walked on but this was one affair too many and he threw her out. She didn't go quietly.'

He turned and smiled mirthlessly for a moment before turning to stare over the garden again. 'She had never really bothered with Mitch and I but she knew how much my father loved his sons and so she fought him in the courts for us. It was an acrimonious time and because my father still loved her it made it doubly hard for him. The courts decided my father should have custody most of the time with my mother having us in the holidays and so on, but even before the divorce was through my father was giving in to her again. She decided one day she was going to whisk us over to England for an extended stay with her parents, but as we were about to board the plane I looked at my father and knew I wanted to stay with him.'

'He was upset, your father?' Robyn asked softly.

'He was crying,' Clay said flatly. 'There was a scene at the airport and the end result was Mitch leaving with my mother and my staying with my father in the States. A week later there was an accident at the farm. Mitch had been driving a tractor in one of the fields—without permission of course—and it turned over on him. He was killed instantly.'

'Oh, Clay.' She was thinking about her own upbringing, the well of love that had been present in her home, and her voice was thick. What would she have done if anything had happened to Cass?

'You would think my mother would have been grief-stricken, wouldn't you?' His hands were thrust deep in his pockets now, his profile hard and cold. 'That's what my father assumed, anyway, and he couldn't wait to get over to her. She put on a good act, the grieving mother and wife, and the divorce was dropped and they got back together again, but she was playing him for a fool within weeks. She was an unnatural mother and the mistress of manipulation: cold, conscienceless and utterly selfish. When my father found out about her latest affair, she managed to turn the tables on him and intimate *he* was responsible for Mitch's being in England, and therefore his death, by wanting a divorce in the first place. More amazingly she got him to believe it.'

He shook his head slowly as though it still filled him with incredulity. 'It did something to him, the guilt, and whatever I said over the next few years it never went away. She used to tell him he was a failure as a husband and a father—' He stopped abruptly, and she saw the broad male chest rise and fall with the force of his emotion.

Robyn was still trying to come to terms with the picture in her mind of a small, confused eleven-year-old boy who had lost his beloved twin brother, and who, instead of being comforted and supported by those nearest to him, had taken on the role of emotional support for his father whilst despising and loathing his mother.

'I hated her.' It was as though he had heard her thoughts. 'If it wasn't for my father's youngest sister, Margo, I don't know how I'd have got through those dark years. She's a wit, Margo.' He turned to look at Robyn suddenly. 'You would like her. She's sharp, funny, direct to the point of rudeness but with a heart of gold underneath. My mother couldn't stand the sight of her—or me. She never forgave me for choosing my father over her.'

He shrugged as though dislodging a weight from his shoulders, and his voice was even and steady when he continued. 'My father died when I was twenty-two, although I think the death blow was dealt by my mother when Mitch died. Three months later I met the girl I married: the daughter of one of my mother's bridge friends. Damn it, I was such a fool.'

'I don't understand?' Robyn was shocked by the savagery in the last words.

'My mother manipulated the whole thing although I didn't see it until much later,' he ground out slowly. 'She recognised a kindred spirit in Laura you see: someone as cold and calculating as herself. Laura could have been her blood daughter. And they liked each other—that should have told me something. Before Laura, my mother had tried to make my girlfriends' lives hell.'

'But didn't you ever suspect Laura was different to how she appeared?' Robyn asked quietly This was Clay Lincoln: he of the razor-sharp mind and ruthless discernment that was a byword in business circles. But then, she reminded herself silently, he had certainly got her all wrong that night out at the lake. *He had thought she was like his mother.* The thought hit her in the stomach with the force of a sledgehammer. And later, when they had first met again at Guy's birthday party.

'I tried to finish the engagement once before we got married.' It was expressionless. 'But it wasn't because I thought Laura was anything other than what she portrayed: sweet, innocent, gentle, kind.'

Everything his mother hadn't been and everything he was craving for, Robyn acknowledged.

'She was devastated, threatened to kill herself and so on, and so…I went through with it, the marriage. I hadn't realised then that the possibility of Laura committing suicide was as likely as a black-widow spider stinging itself to death. They reserve all their venom for their mate.'

'Emotional blackmail, the oldest trick in the world,' Robyn agreed softly.

'However marriage revealed Laura *was* different to my mother in one respect,' Clay continued cynically. 'Whereas one was an alley cat, the other was totally frigid. And the ironic thing, the really funny thing, which must have given my mother a great deal of amusement, was that it was Laura's profession that she wanted to keep herself pure until her wedding night that really hooked me.'

Because of how he had watched his mother behaving all his life. Yes, she could understand that, Robyn thought painfully, her heart aching for him.

'The marriage didn't work?' she asked carefully.

'Didn't work?' He smiled bitterly. 'Oh, I tried to make it work for a time, too long a time. Margo realised I was near to a breakdown one day and got me to tell her the whole story; until then I'd kept it to myself. How do you tell anyone your wife expected to be paid for her favours with diamonds and mink coats, and that even then she'd make you feel you were raping her every time you tried to make love? Sex was a weapon of power to Laura but even when she could bring herself to use it it disgusted her. *I* disgusted her.'

'She was sick, Clay.' Her heart was thudding with the impact of what he had revealed and the knowledge, the terrifying knowledge, that she would never be able to see him as ruthless womaniser and cold man of the world again. And she needed to do that, desperately. It was her only protection against her heart.

'Yes, she was sick,' he agreed quietly. 'But not in a vulnerable, susceptible way. She was a twin soul with my mother in that they were immune to self-doubt, impervious to anyone else's feelings but their own. Unassailable and without conscience. I tell you, Robyn—' he turned to look her full in the face and she felt her breath constrict at the look in the silver eyes '—it's a terrifying thing to live with someone like that, and I've managed it twice. I've seen what love and marriage and commitment can do to a good man like my father, and the only reason I didn't end up crushed and broken like him was because I recognised very early on that I had never known the real Laura. The one I'd married had been a figment of my imagination—or perhaps I should say, hers.'

'She...she died, didn't she?'

He nodded, his profile showing no emotion. 'We were in the middle of divorce proceedings and she'd moved out and gone to live—not with her own parents as one might have expected—but with my mother. They'd called in at my office after a lunch-time at the bridge club and informed me they were really going to take me to the cleaners. Boy, did they enjoy telling me what was in store.' His eyes narrowed at the memory. 'It was probably the last pleasure they had. The car went off the road at a nasty bend, I understand; my mother always drove too fast.'

She truly didn't know what to say. This explained so much but it was so awful, so hard to take in, that she was speechless. She reached forward, touching his arm. 'Some people have happy marriages, Clay. Your mother—' should she say this about his mother, she thought suddenly before her heart said, Go on, say it, it's the truth '—your mother was unnatural, like you said. Every generation has one or two people like that but most people want happy relationships with the person they love.'

'And Laura?' The question was very dry and cynical.

'You were unlucky.' She saw the dark eyebrows rise

derisively and added quickly, 'You *said* she was virtually chosen by your mother and presented in a nice gift-wrapped package your mother knew would appeal. Your mother orchestrated it all really.'

Although how a woman could behave like that to her own son was beyond belief. But then, through the ages, from Roman times and before, there were instances of mothers murdering offspring for position, manoeuvring sons and daughters and sacrificing them for gain or spite, toppling children from thrones and betraying one child in favour of another. Love could be the most powerful force for good in the universe but when it was corrupted...

'So you believe in happy families and two point four children?'

His voice had been scathing and now her small chin lifted in defiance of the mockery. 'When it works, when it's good then it can be very, very good,' she said quietly, 'like with my own parents.'

'And when it doesn't work?' he asked expressionlessly. 'Who is there for the countless casualties, the children, then? Who mends the broken lives, Robyn? Society demands we put a nice clean mask on and get on with the task of living, you know that as well as I do. There are millions of people out there living in a hell of their own making, and the divorce statistics don't even begin to tell the real number.'

'You are like the old man who looked at the sky and saw the rain clouds.' She didn't have the words to fight what he was saying, besides which the cynicism, the pain, was too much to combat. 'Next to them was a gloriously radiant rainbow, and when someone pointed that out to him do you know what he said?'

'Surprise me.'

'That is merely an arch of colours formed by reflection which will shortly disperse, leaving only the rain clouds.'

He eyed her silently for some moments, and Robyn was conscious of a sudden squawk and carrying-on in the privet hedge at the far side of the garden where a group of sparrows were squabbling as to who sat where, before all fell silent and the insects continued their background drone.

'Old man.' His tone was thoughtful. 'Charming!'

'I meant—'

'I know what you meant.' His eyes were pure silver in the mellow light, and sombre, his lips slightly pursed as though in reflection. And then his mouth unexpectedly softened. 'Are you real, Robyn Brett?' he murmured, pulling her towards him so that the smell and feel of him was all about her, teasing at her senses and making her head swim.

'Real enough.' She tried to make it light but instead her voice came out breathless.

'Maybe, maybe not.' He was holding her loosely within the circle of his arms, his hands round her waist and his face looking down into her upturned one. 'For the first time in a long, long while I'm looking forward to being with someone, and I'm not so sure I like that at times.' The comment was almost bewildered and at another time, with someone else, might have been funny. But not now, not with Clay.

Robyn was aware her heart had soared at the reluctant confession which again was a warning in itself, and an odd panicky yet thrilling, excitement had her looking at him wide-eyed, her pupils dilated. His eyes looked back at her, crystal-bright under their thick black lashes and his hard, handsome face dark.

He didn't want to start caring about her. Her heart was

pounding much too fast and she wanted to take a long, deep breath to draw air into her lungs but she didn't dare. Those piercing eyes saw far too much at the best of times.

And she understood the playboy façade now. The two women who should have loved him most in his life—his mother and his wife—had been the very ones to betray him. The first wrecking his childhood and youth, taking his twin brother from him and slowly torturing his father, and the second rejecting and deceiving him, entrapping him in a loveless marriage which had threatened to destroy his mental health. How could he ever open up his eyes to the beauty of the rainbow after all that?

She took hold of her racing thoughts, forcing her voice into the lightness she had tried for earlier as she said quietly, 'It's only you who can decide who you want to be with and how you see your life mapping out, Clay. I'm not going to twist your arm one way or the other.'

'I'd worked that out for myself,' he said with the touch of dryness which was habitual with him. 'Perhaps that's why I've told you more about my past than I'm comfortable with. They say confession is good for the soul but I find the concept of wearing one's heart on one's sleeve a particularly repugnant one.'

'I'd worked that out for myself.' She parried his earlier words with a smile, and was rewarded by a low chuckle. He pulled her into him, kissing her very thoroughly before raising his head again and looking down into her flushed face.

'How much longer are you going to keep up this ridiculous charade?' he drawled easily.

'Charade?' The change from the bitter, angry and hurt individual to the one who was faintly bewildered by the need to be with her had been pretty hard to take, but now this third person—the normal Clay, the Clay who was totally sure of himself and everyone else—hit her on the raw. 'I don't know what you mean,' she prevaricated to give herself time to think.

'You said you wanted time to get to know me,' he reminded her offhandedly, one hand stroking down her hot face and tracing the outline of her mouth, swollen and tingling from his kisses, before his fingers continued to caress her throat. And then his hand moved in a light, tantalising way over her swollen breasts, which ached from the pressure of being held next to his hard male chest, and she had to bite back a low moan of desire as his fingers lingered on one hard peak. 'So, what else do you want to know?' he queried softly.

Now this was pure going-for-the-jugular style, Clay Lincoln. Master strategist and never one to miss an opportunity, Robyn thought with a spurt of healthy anger. She didn't think for a minute he had purposefully revealed all he had about his background with a premeditated idea of using her sympathy to get her into his bed; in fact she suspected he had annoyed himself with just what he *had* said, but that taken as read he still had one ultimate goal in mind—an affair. With everything his own way and on his terms. He was amazing!

The lingering effects of his lovemaking and the tender ache in her heart brought about by his revelations about his past took a nose dive. He was still playing games and working to a formula, she acknowledged bitterly.

'Why do I feel the temperature has suddenly dropped ten degrees?' he drawled silkily.

'Why do I feel I'm being manipulated?' Robyn countered with a sweetness that didn't hide the acid underneath.

'It was worth a try.' He was totally unrepentant, and Robyn went along with the overt mockery to diffuse the overwhelmingly fierce intimacy that always was a breath away when they were alone together.

Over the last weeks she had grown closer to him, and he to her, and they both knew it. She also knew Clay liked that even less than he liked the thought of looking forward to being with her. This was not what he had expected a couple of months ago when he had first decided to renew his old acquaintance with Guy's little sister-in-law, she acknowledged painfully. He'd had her labelled as one of the very cosmopolitan, worldly career women he usually went for. But she hadn't played ball. She still didn't intend to play ball. So…

How long before he cut his losses and moved on?

Mrs Jones called them into the house for their meal in the next moment but, even as they walked back through the lazy evening hand in hand, Robyn was forcing herself to recognise this could only end one way. She mustn't hope for anything else.

As usual the meal was wonderful, and Robyn grimaced ruefully after she finished the last of Mrs Jones's rich chocolate-fudge cake topped by whipped cream and flakes of dark chocolate. 'I'm putting on weight, this has got to stop,' she said regretfully. 'But it's so tempting when it's placed in front of you like this.'

'Quite.'

She looked up and his eyes were smiling, laughing into hers, and she knew he wasn't talking about the dessert. She wrinkled her small nose at him, smiling herself as she said, 'I must phone Cass after we've finished coffee, if that's all right? Guy has had to pop across to France with his job and I promised him I would check Cass is all right each night until he's back. He'll only be gone three days but you'd think he was disappearing on an expedition up the Nile the way he worried about her. She's got weeks to go yet but she's been having the odd niggling pain for the last few days, which the midwife assures her is perfectly normal.'

'No problem.'

He was leaning back in his chair, his pose relaxed and indolent, and Robyn didn't know why her heart suddenly felt as though it was breaking as she looked at him. She loved him so much. She had fought against it since she was sixteen and these last weeks had told her that without Clay in her life the world was a grey place, uninteresting and mundane. And that frightened her more and more as time went on.

She didn't doubt Clay wanted her and was prepared to be patient...for now. But his patience would run out soon; that comment in the garden earlier had confirmed he was getting tired of coaxing her along. Sooner or later there would be a confrontation between them and then this would all end, because she knew now, more than ever, that she could never give herself to him knowing her love wasn't returned. She would simply not survive the aftermath of their affair after he had said goodbye, and each moment they were together before that happened would be tainted by the knowledge of what was to come.

And she didn't want to be one of those sad, jealous women who were for ever looking over their shoulder at every young attractive woman who came within their partner's vision. Suspecting this nubile flirt or that, watching for the moment when something sparked between Clay and someone else, anticipating it, dreading it. Maybe she would last a month or two, even a year or two—who knew? But eventually would come the day when he would begin to retreat from her, become preoccupied...

'What's the matter?' Clay leant forward suddenly

across the table, taking her hand in his before she could draw away. 'What were you thinking about just then?'

'Nothing.' It was quick and defensive, and Robyn was heartily thankful when Mrs Jones chose that precise moment to bustle in with the coffee pot and a plate of her delicious shortbread. A heart to heart tonight was definitely not what she needed.

Clay looked up at his housekeeper, his voice pleasant and his expression easy when he said, 'We'll have a tray in the sitting room please, Mrs Jones, and then you get off to bed. Leave the clearing up till the morning.'

As they walked through to the sitting room he said in an undertone to Robyn, his breath on her ear making her insides curl with sexual tension, 'Mr Jones was unwell last night and she was up half the night with him.'

'Oh, I'm sorry.'

'Just in case you thought I had an ulterior motive in getting rid of her,' he added smoothly, his warm hand on her elbow sending shivers flickering down her spine and causing her to miss her step so she fell against him, twisting her ankle in the process.

It wasn't a bad sprain, hardly anything at all, but once Mrs Jones had delivered the coffee tray Clay insisted on settling her on one of the sofas before kneeling down in front of her and taking off her sandal, despite Robyn's protests that she was perfectly all right.

'Does that hurt?' he asked softly.

He had been running his fingers over her foot, his flesh warm against her silken skin, and in her reclining position Robyn felt extremely vulnerable and ridiculously excited. His touch was delicate, sensual, and with his dark head on a level with hers and his broad muscled shoulders flexing and moving under the silk shirt she found her mouth had gone dry.

She wet her lips surreptitiously, trying to speak normally when she said, 'It's fine.'

'Are you sure?' he drawled, his accent lazy on the air.

Oh, for crying out loud, *stop*. She was only human wasn't she? He must know what he was doing to her. 'Yes.'

His hands had slid just above her ankle, continuing their slow massage of the tight, locked muscles they encountered, but even though Robyn was aware he must realise she was as tense as a coiled spring she couldn't relax an iota.

She wanted to moan at what his hands were doing as they travelled further up her leg, caressing her calf, her knee, and then stroking over the soft skin on her lower thigh.

'Clay, please.' She gasped the protest that wasn't a protest at all, as he stretched over her, both hands now sliding to her thighs as his eyes locked with hers.

'You're so beautiful, Robyn.' His voice was husky and uneven and she felt her heated skin would catch fire if he didn't stop. 'I dream about you, do you know that? The smell of you, the taste of you, how it will be. I want you, I want you now.'

Twilight had fallen while they had been eating and the open French windows allowed the faintest of breezes to gently waft the scent of roses into the room, the shadows of the dying day creating a warm intimacy that was intoxicating. Robyn was unable to move, unable to stop what she knew was going to happen next.

He rolled in one swift movement and she found herself lying on top of him on the sofa, the thrusting arousal of his body hard and very real against the softness of her belly. He captured the gasp of shock on her half-open lips with his mouth, his hands sliding over her hips and holding her fast against him.

His tongue flicked against her teeth before slowly and surely exploring the sweet, secret places of her mouth, and in spite of herself Robyn was kissing him back, her hands coming up to cradle his face as her lips became as hungry as his.

She was aching and melting inside, her breasts painful with the swollen need she was feeling and she could feel herself shaking against the hard wall of his chest. Her fingers fumbled with the small buttons in the silk, and then the broad expanse of his tanned, muscled chest was exposed as the shirt swung open. The light covering of dark silky body hair was soft beneath her fingers as her hands explored his body, tentatively, wonderingly at first, and then, as more and more sensation built, she became bolder.

His hands and mouth were fuelling and feeding the abandonment, his thighs hard against hers as he branded her with his maleness and then he stilled, his whole body tensing as she lowered her head and shyly ran her warm tongue over the taut, pea-sized nodules of his nipples.

His kiss was fiercer and hungrier when she raised her head and he took her lips again, and Robyn matched him in desire. He was so beautiful; every inch of him was beautiful and she would never make love with anyone if she didn't make love with Clay, she told herself feverishly. It would be unthinkable to let another man touch her, kiss her like this.

How long they touched and tasted each other Robyn wasn't sure afterwards—it could have been seconds or minutes or hours, such was her intoxication—but when she felt his hands pulling at her dress, the skirt of which had ridden up high against her thighs, refusing him didn't enter her mind.

And then she realised he was smoothing her skirt down as he lifted her off him, his voice husky as he said, 'Come upstairs, Robyn. I want our first time to be long and slow and pleasurable, not a quick, lusty coupling on the sofa.'

'What?' The feverish agony of need that had consumed her made her voice dazed and plaintive, and then, as he repeated, 'We're going to bed and I want you to stay the night,' she gazed at him bewilderly.

He looked back at her, the silver gaze steady and controlled despite the passion that had narrowed his eyes and had brought a dark streak of colour across his chiselled cheekbones, and suddenly, shockingly, she knew exactly what he was doing.

He had told her that when she finally went to bed with him it would be because she had chosen to do so because she wanted him as much as he wanted her. Eyes wide open, his conditions met and accepted, no surge of emotion, sexual or otherwise, blurring the issue.

She suddenly felt sick. And she would become his slave. Loving him as she did, she would become his slave, because if ever a relationship was one-sided this one was. He thought she had been nervous about a physical relationship because of a bad experience in the past, and that once she had grown to like him and accept all the advantages an affair with a man like himself could bring, she would be content to relax and have fun for as long as it lasted. Surface emotion, nothing too deep or uncomfortable.

She struggled off the sofa and then stood swaying slightly, her head whirling, and when he rose swiftly to his feet and took her arms in his she didn't shrug him away for the simple reason that she felt she would collapse in front of him if she did. It was only moments and then the faintness had receded, and when he looked down at her, his voice a mixture of concern and surprise and something else she couldn't fathom, he said, 'Robyn? What is it?' She breathed deeply before she spoke.

'Let go of me, Clay.' Her voice was small but firm.

'What?' His eyes narrowed, darkened.

'I said let go of me.' Whatever he had expected her to say, it wasn't this, she realised grimly, as his hands dropped from her arms.

'Are you ill?' he asked carefully.

'No, I'm not ill.' He looked magnificent standing there, her heart cried out desperately; the blue silk shirt open to the waist and his thickly muscled torso and lean, strong shoulders tanned and flagrantly male. 'I just have to leave, that's all.'

'Leave?' He repeated the word almost uncomprehendingly, a small muscle jerking under one high cheekbone. 'What the hell are you talking about?'

'I can't stay here and spend the night with you, Clay. Not now, not at any time,' she said very clearly, considering her insides had broken loose from their casing and her heart was jangling about in a million pieces.

'The hell you can't.' His eyes raked over her white face, their piercing quality threatening to strip her to the bone. 'That was you lying next to me a minute ago, Robyn. Your lips murmuring my name and asking me, begging me, to relieve your torment.'

Had she? She seemed to remember that other woman, the one that had been alive until a few moments ago, doing what he had said. She nodded slowly. 'I know.'

He stared at her, his eyes running over her stiff countenance and the frantic pulse beating at the base of her slender throat. 'So what's changed in a minute or two?'

he asked evenly, his voice cool. 'You're still the same woman, I'm still the same man.'

She stared back at him and then answered his question with one of her own. 'You don't like emotion, do you, Clay?' she said quietly, her voice small but very clear. 'Emotion smacks of letting go, of not being in control, doesn't it?'

'We're not discussing my likes or dislikes,' he said harshly.

'All your childhood was made up of emotion: highs and lows that swept you along from one crisis to the next. One minute hoping everything would be all right between your parents and seeing your father happy for a while, then the next back to your grandparents while another catastrophe was dealt with. Then after Mitch's death things got even worse until the final meltdown when your father died. Then along came Laura.'

'Is there a point to this?'

His hard voice made her wince inside but she didn't reveal it to the crystal gaze watching her. 'You must have craved peace of mind by then, a life of dignity and restraint after the war zone you'd lived in most of your life.'

'You know nothing about me so cut the psychoanalysis,' he said with a sharpness that told her she was getting to him.

'But I do know quite a lot about you, Clay, don't I?' she said quietly, her face as pale as alabaster. She knew he wouldn't like being reminded of the fact but she had nothing to lose now; this was goodbye whichever way she looked at it. 'And with Laura came more furore and heartache, possibly the worst yet, or maybe losing Mitch or seeing your father die inch by inch over the years was the worst thing—I don't know.'

'You mean there's actually something about me you

think you don't know?' he said with acid sarcasm. 'How refreshing!'

'And so after Laura and your mother died and you were released from it all for the first time in your life, you determined that never again would you put yourself in a position where passion or sentiment or desire or love could govern you. You would always be in control, always call the tune, be it business or your personal life.' Her eyes were huge as she stared into his face.

He was looking at her as though he hated her, and that more than anything else told her she was forcing him to acknowledge the demons that sat on his shoulders. And he would never forgive her for this, for showing him that she understood what he considered his Achilles heel.

'And so you live your life in a cold, dispassionate vacuum, unmoved and detached from the things that touch the rest of us poor mortals, and in the final analysis, when you look at it with the cold logic you're so proud of, you have to acknowledge that Laura and your mother have won. They've accomplished what they set out to do: dominated your thinking and mastered your life.'

'The hell they have.'

'Think about it, Clay,' she said sadly. 'Just think about it. They're still with you, holding you back, stifling you.'

'I don't have to think about such rubbish,' he bit out furiously, the cool control that he prided himself on blown to the wind. 'The same as I don't have to think about the motive behind that little précis of my life. It's all with one object in view, isn't it? A ring on your finger before you consent to sleep with me. Don't think I'm a fool, Robyn, because I am not. I'm on to your little game.'

'If you believe that then there is nothing else left to say,' she said with touching dignity, her chin jerking up and her eyes flashing as she faced him head-on. His contempt had sent a rush of adrenalin surging through her veins, and she welcomed the boost of hormone from the bottom of her heart as it enabled her to confront him without flinching. 'And you are a fool, Clay Lincoln. A blind, pathetic fool.'

'Have you quite finished?'

She got the feeling from the ice in his eyes that if she touched him now it would be like touching liquid nitrogen, so cold was his face. 'Yes, I'm finished,' she said woodenly.

She turned from him, reaching for her bag at the side of the sofa, and as she did so her mobile phone began to ring. 'Do you mind?' She indicated the phone, the process of retrieving it out of the bag making her realise just how badly she was trembling.

He shook his head, his face saying all too clearly he didn't care what she did as long as she was soon out of his sight.

It took two attempts before her shaking fingers could negotiate the right button, but then she was speaking her name into the phone and listening to Cass's agitated voice. 'Don't worry, I'll be with you as soon as I can. Stay put and let the twins sleep till I get there,' she said urgently after a moment.

She pressed the button to finish the call and glanced up at Clay who was staring at her. 'I need to call a taxi,' she said frantically. 'It's Cass; the baby's coming and it's weeks early.'

CHAPTER EIGHT

OVER the next little while Robyn saw first-hand the qualities which had made Clay into a multimillionaire in his own right, as he took charge of events with a smooth authority that was formidable.

The journey from Windsor into central London down the M4 was accomplished in half the legal time, as Clay's car—the Mercedes this time—flashed through the night at a speed which took Robyn's breath away.

Not that she had much breath left anyway. The caustic scene at the house followed by Cass's distraught telephone call had settled like a hard, tight ball in Robyn's chest, constricting her breathing and causing her to feel she was in the middle of a nightmare she couldn't wake up from.

Fifteen minutes after speaking to her sister on the phone Robyn was holding Cass in her arms, and there was no doubt the baby was on its way, early or not. Although the contractions weren't following any particular pattern Cass's waters had broken.

'There's no need to panic.' Now the other two were here and she wasn't alone with the twins, Cass had visibly relaxed, the tearful face which had greeted Clay and Robyn now calmer. 'The twins took for ever to be born. It's just the fact that the baby is coming so early that's worrying me.'

'Didn't I read somewhere that second labours are often shorter though?' Robyn asked anxiously, and no sooner had the words left her lips than a new contraction hit with enough force to make Cass pant like an animal as she held on to Robyn's hand with a grip that would have done credit to a twenty-stone navvy.

Once Clay had established Cass had contacted Guy and Guy was on his way to the airport where he'd been squeezed onto a flight leaving just before one o'clock, he popped round to pick up Guy's brother's wife—who would stay with the twins until Guy arrived at the hospital and Robyn could come and hold the fort with her nephews—while Robyn hastily packed her sister's overnight case.

'I was going to do all this in the next week or so,' Cass said plaintively as she directed Robyn into drawers and wardrobe. 'Oh, Robyn, the baby'll be all right, won't it?'

'Of course it will,' Robyn said stoutly. It had to be. It just had to be. 'Just tell it to slow down a bit so Daddy can see it arrive, will you?' she added with an attempt at lightness.

'You were at Clay's, then?' Cass asked with elaborate offhandedness. 'Had dinner there or something?'

'Uh-huh.' Now was not the time to tell Cass her little fantasy had come to a sad end, although Robyn had noticed that not once, since they had left Clay's house, had he looked directly at her. It was as though he couldn't bear to acknowledge her presence.

That Cass had picked up something too was made clear in the next moment when she said, 'You two weren't in the middle of a row or something, were you?' Her tone was tentative.

'No.' They hadn't been—they'd just finished. 'I was just going to leave actually.' It was brisk and dismissive.

'Right.' Robyn could tell Cass wasn't convinced but then another contraction gripped, stronger this time, and within moments all her sister's concentration was focused on her breathing exercises as she battled with the clamp on her belly.

By the time Clay brought Beryl in the front door Robyn and Cass were sitting waiting in the lounge and the contractions were coming every six minutes. As the three of them went to leave, Cass groaned. 'Oh no, not another', she said, and went to lean against the door stanchion, but Clay whisked her up in his arms, his voice not quite his own as he said, 'Come on, come on, we need to get you to the hospital. Do that panting thing or whatever it is you do.'

He was panicking. The knowledge was so surprising that Robyn almost dropped Cass's overnight bag. He was actually behaving like a normal human being for once. She had never thought to see the cool, smooth, controlled Clay Lincoln running to his car like a greyhound with a very rotund Cass in his arms, but she was seeing it now.

In the moment that Clay bent down and slid Cass into the back seat Robyn caught her sister's eye, and she saw by the wry expression on Cass's face her sister's thoughts had been parallel with her own. And in spite of the dire circumstances—for herself as well as Cass—Robyn found herself smiling as Cass winked at her. This was very different to his business world.

They shot through the streets again but this time Robyn was sitting in the back of the car with Cass. Her sister's fingernails were biting into the flesh of Robyn's hands with each contraction but Robyn scarcely noticed. All her energy was directed at encouraging Cass along and keeping her eyes off the dark figure in the driving seat.

She couldn't believe it was over. She suddenly wanted to cry, hot tears pricking at the back of her eyes, and she forced her mind back to the matter in hand, namely her sister. She had to help Cass through the next few hours, nothing mattered beyond that. She could think about Clay and the way it had ended later. She was going to have a lot of spare time in which to think now.

When they arrived at the hospital Clay had everyone jumping around as though they were on springs, until the sister in charge of the maternity unit—a large lady with a face like a sergeant major—ascertained that no, he wasn't the father and yes, Mrs Barnes would like a bit of peace and quiet, and banished him to the waiting area while they examined the mother-to-be. 'Please pipe down, Mr Lincoln,' she said pleasantly but very firmly. 'I can assure you we will look after your friend's wife to the very best of our ability and we have been doing this job for quite a while. I can understand you feel responsible for Mrs Barnes until her husband gets here, but panicking won't help the patient, now will it?'

Robyn was witness to this little exchange and accompanied Clay to the waiting area whilst Cass was admitted and found a bed in one of the delivery rooms, her head still trying to take on board that someone had actually had the temerity to tell Clay Lincoln to pipe down. All things considered this really wasn't his night, was it? she told herself with a touch of silent hysteria.

Thankfully there were one or two other people in the waiting area which had comfortable chairs and tables, plenty of magazines and a couple of machines serving hot and cold drinks and snacks. It made the frozen silence emanating from Clay easier to ignore.

Within a few minutes Sister Robinson was back to inform them that Cass was doing fine and would like Robyn to join her in the delivery room if she so wished? Robyn did so wish and, after receiving directions to the appropriate delivery room, she left the sister being quizzed by Clay on exactly what was happening concerning the birth.

The sister seemed to be taking this in good part and answering him patiently and concisely, but it was clear she wasn't in awe of her interrogator.

As luck would have it Cass's daughter hung on to be born till five minutes after Guy had arrived, and so it was that Samantha Robyn came into the world with her father and her aunty in attendance as they urged her mother on.

She was a beautiful baby, very small at exactly four pounds but with a healthy pair of lungs that were exercised until the moment she was placed at her mother's breast whereupon she settled down with a contented sigh as though to say, This is all I wanted; I'm all right now. Robyn fell in love with her on sight.

After hugs and kisses and more hugs and kisses, Robyn left Cass and Guy with their new baby daughter after promising them she would go straight to their home and take care of the boys until Cass was home again. 'Drew and Fiona will hold the fort for a couple of days,' she said airily as though the mountain of work that was ever present was of no account at all. Which, after the miracle she'd seen that morning, was quite true. 'And Mum and Dad have already booked their flight out and will be here on Friday to look after things for a couple of weeks, which will give Guy time to arrange to bring his holiday forward.'

'Bless you, Robyn.' Cass's eyes had been full, and the two sisters had hugged again before Robyn had let herself out of the room in order to send Clay to see the baby before they left.

She stood for a moment, the joy and happiness contained in the room behind her at stark contrast with what she was going to have to face in a few moments. And then she squared her slim shoulders and walked along to the waiting area which was now quite empty apart from the tall, lean man lying dozing in one of the big chairs, and several empty paper cups which had clearly contained coffee on the table beside him.

She walked quietly across to the side of Clay's chair, her feet making no sound on the thin cord carpet, and stood looking down at him for a moment.

The harsh male face was younger in repose, softer, the hard cynical lines that cut through the tanned skin when he was awake barely visible.

He would look like this in the morning before he was awake, Robyn thought despairingly as her love for him welled up in a flood. Had she made the worst mistake of her life by refusing to stay last night? Could it have been the start of something that would have lasted despite everything he had said to the contrary? Maybe she would have grown on him, woven herself into the fabric of his life until he couldn't have done without her? Perhaps he might even have come to love her?

And then she caught the pain and regret and panic that had her heart thudding and her stomach churning. There were too many maybes and perhaps, she told herself wearily. Far, far too many. Reality was that he had made his choice years ago on how he wanted to live his life and it would take someone very special, someone with far more experience of love and life than she had, to break through the steel casing he'd erected round his heart. Perhaps such a person didn't exist. If nothing else Clay was not a person who changed his mind lightly on anything, and this was a fundamental part of what made him him. She had done the only thing she could in the circumstances. Anything else would have been emotional suicide.

'Goodbye, my darling.' She whispered the words on the lightest of breaths, her eyes stinging with the tears she had kept at bay for so long. 'I love you, I'll always love you, and I pray one day you'll be happy, that you'll find the peace of mind you need so badly. I wish I could have been the one to set you free.'

She had to go and wash her face before she woke him to tell him Cass and Guy were waiting to show him the baby. She stumbled out of the room, her face awash, but after a minute or two in the ladies' cloakroom and with a gallon of cold water splashed on her face the red blotches were gone and she looked pale but normal.

When she braced herself to return to the waiting area Clay was gone, and after retracing her footsteps she found him in the delivery room with Cass and Guy and the baby.

'Here she is.' Guy's voice was hearty as Robyn popped her head round the door. 'We wondered where you were.'

'I went to the ladies' cloakroom,' Robyn said, adding quickly, 'I was going to come and tell you about the baby, Clay, afterwards but you were already in here.' She didn't want him thinking she bore him some grudge and out of spite hadn't fetched him. The way he had looked at her earlier she feared he wouldn't put anything past her, and his track record with women hadn't exactly led him to assume that finer feelings dominated their thinking!

His eyes had been on Cass and the baby nestled in her arms when Robyn had opened the door, but now he glanced up from his position of sitting at the end of the bed, and she saw he was looking positively stunned. It touched her more than words could say. He was clearly bowled over by the tiny new life in front of him, and as he just nodded in answer she saw he was at a loss for words.

'We've just said to Clay that we want you two to be her godparents,' Cass said eagerly, and then, without waiting for a response from Robyn, she said to Clay, 'Come on, then, have a hold before Sister Robinson comes back and whisks her away. She's going to spend the night in an incubator just to be on the safe side because she's so tiny, although they've said everything is absolutely fine and there are no problems.'

Seeing him with that tiny little bundle cradled in his arms would be too much to cope with. Robyn knew her limits, and her suddenly weeping and wailing wouldn't exactly add to the wonder of the moment.

As Clay rose to take Samantha Robyn, Robyn said hastily, 'I'll get myself a quick coffee; it might lessen the sister's wrath if the room isn't too crowded when she comes back. I'll come back later tonight for a few minutes, Cass, if Beryl will babysit for an hour,' and she shut the door quickly before her sister called for her to stay.

It was another ten minutes before Clay joined her in the waiting area, and two cups of strong black coffee enabled Robyn to adopt a fairly neutral expression as she looked into the hard, handsome face and said quietly, 'I can get a taxi from here, Clay, if you want to get off home and change before you go to work.'

He glanced at her briefly as he shook his head. 'I'll take you home so you can pick up a few things and then take you to Guy's,' he said briefly as she followed him out into the corridor.

He said nothing more as they walked through the quiet hospital most of which was still sleeping, and Robyn couldn't bring herself to break the silence which was taut and painful now they were alone. A silence that was piercing her heart.

She couldn't quite decide how he had looked when he had come into the waiting area. Certainly the furious rage and contempt and bitter condemnation with which he had viewed her after their altercation at his house was gone, neither were his eyes shooting ice-cold shafts as they had done when they'd met hers in the hours at the hospital before the baby was born, when she'd visited the waiting area a few times to keep him up-to-date on developments.

Perhaps the stunned wonder which had verged on disbelief that she had seen on his face in the delivery room when he'd looked at Samantha had mellowed him a little? Enough for him to be civil anyway? She hoped so; she didn't think she could take much more.

Her thoughts were so tied up with Clay and she was so tired after the long night that she almost walked into the wall of the corridor at one point, and as his hand came out to steady her and he said, 'Careful, you must be exhausted,' their eyes met for a moment before his hand dropped away and they continued to the big glass doors that led to the hospital car park.

It was a cold, distant mask that she had seen. The knowledge kept her working on automatic as they stepped out of the vaguely antiseptic anonymity of the hospital into the fresh, clean beauty of the early morning. An uninterested face and indifferent eyes.

A pale gold and mother-of-pearl dawn was banishing the last of the night sky and somewhere close by in one of the trees surrounding the car park a missel thrust was singing its heart out to the new day. The summer morning was balmy, promising a hot day, and after the wildly emotional content of the last hours the beauty was almost too much for Robyn's fragile equilibrium.

He didn't care about her, he had never cared about her or else he couldn't have dismissed her so quickly from his heart. Heart? He didn't have a heart, she told herself savagely, the memory of the cold indifference in his face cutting her in two and making her chest ache before she warned herself not to dwell on it, not now. She had the twins to see to, chores to do, a household to run. Thinking could come later, much later.

Once in the car she was vitally conscious of the big male frame next to her, her feelings so sensitised that every tiny movement of the muscled body brought her nerves quivering in response. She had noticed, in the lightning glance they'd exchanged, that his normally immaculate hair had been rumpled and that he had a healthy growth of stubble darkening his face. It had made him look twice as sexy and ten times more dangerous, and now she couldn't get the image out of her mind even though she kept her gaze very firmly on the windscreen.

Once the Mercedes drew up outside her house Robyn turned her head and looked at him, keeping her feelings under wraps as she said formally, 'Would you like to come in for a coffee while I get my things together?'

'I'll wait here. You aren't going to be long, are you?'

'No, of course not.' And as he made a movement to open his door she said curtly, 'I'm quite capable of opening my own door, thank you,' and slid out of the car before he could respond.

She inserted the key into the front door with a hand that trembled, willing herself not to give way, and then the door was open and she almost fell into the quiet, still room beyond, shutting the door and then leaning against it before slowly sliding onto the floor as the tears came.

She had to get control, she had to. Oh, please, God, let me get control. I have to get through the next hour or so with some dignity; it's all I've got left.

Whether the prayer worked or not she didn't know, but somehow she felt able to get up off the floor and drag herself upstairs into the bathroom where she again washed her face, combed her hair and tidied it into a French pleat, before quickly changing her clothes and donning a light summer top and old jeans. That done she flung a few necessities into an overnight bag and quickly ran downstairs again, scribbling a note to Drew along with a list of instructions and her telephone number at Cass's which she placed on her friend's desk. Drew had her own key for use when Robyn wasn't around, so that was no problem.

She was out in the street again within fifteen minutes and already the city was stirring although it was still only just gone five o'clock.

Clay leant across and opened her door for her as she reached the Mercedes and she slid into the passenger seat without looking at him, her face stiff. Okay, so she loved him more than life itself but she was blowed if she was going to beg and plead for a kind word like a whipped puppy, the rat.

The rat glanced at her. 'Cass's?' he asked succinctly.

Robyn kept her gaze directed in front and nodded tightly. 'Thank you,' she said grimly.

It was probably the worst, the most miserable few minutes of her entire life but eventually it was over and the Mercedes was outside Cass's brightly painted little house. Robyn's mouth was dry, her heart pounding much too fast and her tortured senses at breaking point. She breathed deeply and then, as Clay cut the engine, said abruptly, 'Thank you for the lift. Goodbye, Clay.' He hadn't wanted to come in for a few minutes at her house and no power on earth was going to get him through the door of Cass's house as far as she was concerned. 'I'll send Beryl out immediately; I presume you don't mind taking her home?'

There was a moment's pause before he said, his voice cool and faintly quizzical. 'Not at all. I'll wait here, then.'

Yes, you damn well will. She glanced at him then, just

one swift look as she said, 'She'll be out directly.' And then she opened her door, gathered up the overnight bag and was out on the pavement.

He was going to let her go; it was really going to finish as badly as this. Robyn still couldn't quite take it in even as she marched up the path and opened the door with the key Guy had given her at the hospital. As it swung open there was a split second where she almost turned round for one last look at Clay, but she mastered the desire immediately.

If hc looked at her, if there was just a minute softening of that formidable hardness in his face, she might disgrace herself and run to the car and beg him to forgive all the things she had said. Implore him to take her on any terms he cared to dictate.

But she had spoken the truth. And she loved him too much to pretend. And life with Clay on his terms would be one big pretence.

She pulled the door shut behind her, took a hard pull of air, painted a bright smile on her face and walked quietly into the lounge to tell Beryl she was an aunty again.

CHAPTER NINE

Six days later Robyn was seated at her desk at seven in the evening eating a sandwich—which was masquerading as dinner—while she read through some draft copies of a batch of press releases Fiona had written earlier in the day. They were good, they were very good, Robyn decided with some satisfaction. Fiona was going to work out just fine.

When the telephone at her elbow rang she picked it up and said crisply, 'Brett PR. How can I help you?' She had been all on edge the couple of days she had spent at Cass's looking after the twins thinking Clay might ring. And then once her parents had arrived on Friday morning just an hour before their eldest daughter had returned home with their latest grandchild, and she had come to her own house, she had been even more jittery. But he hadn't rung. She knew now he wasn't going to. She was old history as far as Clay was concerned.

'Is that Miss Brett speaking?'

The female voice was American and Robyn frowned in surprise before she answered yes, 'Yes, it is. Can I help you?'

'I really don't know, Miss Brett, but I had to call. This is Margo Bower, Clay's aunt. I don't know if he has mentioned me at all?'

For a moment Robyn could only stare at the receiver, utterly dumbfounded, and then she managed to collect herself and say carefully, 'Yes, Mrs Bower, he has.'

'Oh, good; at least you were aware of my existence,

then.' There was a split second pause and then Clay's aunt continued, 'You are probably wondering why on earth I've rung you and I would be the first to admit it's most presumptuous, but I wondered if I could call round and see you for a few moments, Miss Brett.'

'Call round?' Robyn hoped she didn't sound as taken aback as she felt.

'I'm in England for a day or so,' Margaret Bower informed her briskly. 'A very short vacation of sorts.'

'I see.' No, she didn't, she didn't see at all, and she was not going to be pushed around by anyone ever again. Robyn stared at the ham sandwich hanging limply in her hand and said firmly, 'Mrs Bower, I don't want to be rude but why on earth would you want to come and see me?'

She had cried herself to sleep every night since the day baby Samantha had been born and had averaged about three hours sleep a night before she'd wake, sitting at the window and watching the dawn slowly rise in an uncaring, silent world, before she'd loaded her day with work, work and more work to stop her mind from thinking about this woman's nephew. And now here was Clay's aunt demanding an audience, because that was what this boiled down to. She had had *enough* of this family! Who did they think they were anyway?

There was a longer pause this time, and then the older woman's voice came very quietly. 'Because I'm worried to death about Clay and I need to talk to someone about it.'

'But...your husband? Clay's friends? I'm sure there must be someone more suitable than me,' Robyn protested quietly.

'You, Miss Brett. I need to talk to you,' Margo Bower said flatly. 'I'm actually sitting outside your house right now and I promise you I won't take up more than a few minutes of your time.'

She just didn't believe this, but then it was typical of the Lincoln bulldozer-type approach, Robyn thought bitterly. Although of course this woman was a Bower by marriage, she had the Lincoln blood running through her veins all right.

And then all her misgivings and annoyance was swept away when Margo Bower said in a very small voice that was quite unlike the rather self-assured tone she'd adopted to date, 'Please, Miss Brett?'

The last thing—the very last thing—she wanted to do was to talk to Clay's aunt about anything, so why did she find herself saying, 'Very well, Mrs Bower, if you think it will help you.'

When the knock came on the door and Robyn opened it, a tall, good-looking, well-dressed woman was standing there, her immaculately coiffured hair dyed a discreet mid-brown which made her appear younger than she was for a few moments, until one really looked into the attractive face. 'Miss Brett?'

'Call me Robyn,' Robyn said quietly as she shook the other woman's hand and stood aside for her to enter. 'Come upstairs. Would you like a cup of tea or coffee, or maybe a cold drink?'

'Coffee, if it's not too much trouble.'

When they reached the first floor Robyn waved her visitor upstairs as she said, 'Make yourself comfortable and I'll bring the coffee up in a moment,' and then all thought of coffee was forgotten when Margo Bower said, 'How long have you known my nephew, Robyn?'

Robyn jerked round to face a pair of shrewd blue eyes. 'I first knew him as a young teenager but then we lost touch until a few months ago,' she said stiffly. 'Why?'

'Because I've never seen him like he's been the last little while,' Margo answered very directly. 'I thought...' And then she flapped her hand at herself. 'It doesn't matter what I thought,' she said a touch irritably. 'Did you finish it or him?' And then before Robyn could answer, 'I'm sorry. Really, I'm sorry. You must think this is the height of bad taste but I've always looked on myself more as Clay's mother than his aunt, although that still doesn't excuse my poking my nose into his private life.'

She looked at Robyn with an almost comical air of despair and suddenly Robyn found herself softening. She liked this woman. 'I take it Clay doesn't know you're here?' she said a touch drily.

'Good grief, no.' Margo looked absolutely horrified 'He would never forgive me and I mean that. I've got no excuse, other than that he means a great deal to me. And...and he's had a rotten deal in certain areas of his life.'

Robyn nodded. 'He's told me about his childhood and then his marriage to Laura,' she said quietly.

'He has?' Margo's mouth had dropped open in a little gape. 'However did you get him to do that? To my knowledge he has never confided in a soul apart from me.'

Robyn turned back to the coffee pot. Something told her this wasn't going to be the quick five-minute visit that Clay's aunt had intimated.

Margo stayed for three hours, and by the time she rose to leave the two women were friends.

Robyn had found herself telling Clay's aunt the whole story—apart from the fact that she loved him—and then even that came out when Margo said, very softly, 'You love him, Robyn, don't you? Don't worry, I won't betray a confidence, my dear. But he is a fool. I love him dearly, but I have to say he is a fool. But you could never tell Clay anything from when he was a boy.'

'I told him plenty,' Robyn said a touch wryly.

'So you did, my dear, so you did.'

'And he'll never forgive me for it.' It was something of a wail.

'Never is a long, long time,' Margo said thoughtfully. 'When he came back to the States last Wednesday I've never seen him in such a mood. Oh, I don't mean angry, not exactly, but it was as though something was tearing him apart inside. Many years ago now I remember something similar but this was much, much worse. That's when I made up my mind to find out what had happened and come and see you for myself. I asked after you, you see—he's mentioned you often over the last weeks—and he nearly bit my head off. So, I told him I had a little business to do in France—quite true as it happens—and that I intended to combine the trip with a couple of days sightseeing, and flew out over the weekend. Do you know I'm actually in Paris right now?' she added with a sly smile.

'Clever you.' Robyn smiled back. And then the smile faded as she said, 'But don't assume he cares for me like I do him, Margo, because he doesn't. It was a physical thing on his side mainly. Oh, I don't doubt he grew to like me over the last weeks but there's a vast difference between that and love, isn't there? He was probably upset because of what I said to him, not that our relationship— such as it was—is over.'

'Maybe.' Margo looked at her with sympathetic eyes. 'But don't forget he has had years of hiding his feelings, Robyn, from when he was a little boy in fact. He's all locked up inside.'

The two women hugged as Margo left. 'I shan't mention I've been here,' Margo said quietly as they stood on the doorstep. 'But if I don't see you again, can I just say I think you're one in a million and that I would very much have liked to welcome you into the family.'

'Thank you.' Robyn blinked back the tears until Margo's taxi had disappeared from view, and then she stepped back into the house and had a good howl. That goodbye had sounded terribly final somehow, and seemed to confirm—although Margo hadn't actually said as much—that Clay's aunt saw things the way Robyn did. With the facts as they were it was the *only* way to see things.

She walked up to the kitchen and made a fresh pot of coffee, pouring herself a cup before retracing her way downstairs again.

It was useless to try to go to bed for a while; her head was spinning with all that had been said and the dull ache in her heart told her she wouldn't be able to fight the thoughts of Clay that would swamp her immediately as she laid her head on the pillow. And she was sick to death of crying herself to sleep.

Work, the panacea, as she had proven over the last few days. It might not cure all ills, but at least by the time she fell into bed after working into the early hours she was too exhausted to do more than have a little cry before sleep claimed her for two or three hours, and tonight, maybe, she might even get the victory over that? Because she couldn't carry on like this.

It was gone midnight when the knock came at the front door, startling her so much that half a cup of stale coffee went flying over the papers on the desk.

'Damn, damn, damn!' Her heart was thudding as she whisked the papers up and shook them—the best she could do in the circumstances—but then, when the knock came again, she put them on Drew's desk and her hand went to her throat.

Who on earth would be standing outside at this time of night? she asked herself nervously. Admittedly burglars didn't normally knock to gain entrance, but one heard such funny things these days with kids high on drugs and so on. What should she do? She continued to stand there, her eyes fixed on the front door.

On the third time of knocking, Robyn walked warily to the door and called loudly, 'Yes, who is it?'

There was silence for what seemed like an eternity but in reality was no more than a second or two, and then an unmistakably deep, husky voice said, 'Clay.'

She stood frozen to the spot, her heart thumping so hard it actually hurt and her mind unable to take it in until his voice came again, slightly irate this time. 'Robyn? It's Clay. Can you hear me? Open the door; it's all right.'

He was here. She glanced wildly about the room as though it would provide the answer as to why Clay Lincoln was standing outside her front door in the middle of the night, and then nerved herself to reach up and turn the knob, still not really believing he would be standing outside.

He was.

She saw his eyes narrow as they took in her slim figure encased in the cream shot-silk chiffon dress she had worn for a meeting with an important client earlier in the day and had not bothered to change once she was home again, his gaze lingering on her hair—which she had loosened out of its clip on top of her head and had allowed to cascade free some time during Margo's visit. 'Hello, Robyn.' His voice was deep and husky.

She didn't answer, *couldn't* answer, and the silver gaze

slanted still more as he said, 'Can I come in or do you have a visitor?' as he glanced behind her into the room.

'A visitor?' she repeated breathlessly.

'I saw the lights were still on and assumed you were up, but if you have guests...'

'I was working.' It suddenly clicked that he suspected she had a man here and her voice was curt, even as she thought, It would have served him right if I had.

'So, can I come in?' he repeated quietly. 'We need to talk.'

She stood aside for him to enter, hoping with all her being that she didn't look as poleaxed as she felt at the sight of him. He was wearing a pale grey shirt and black jeans and he took her breath away. But he looked tired too, ill almost.

'What do you want, Clay?' As she turned to face him after shutting the door she was amazed her voice sounded so calm and ordinary when her nerves were jangling and she could feel the blood pounding through her veins. 'It's very late.'

'I know.' He hadn't moved a muscle after stepping into the room and now he surveyed her with unblinking eyes. 'You look tired.'

Did he mean she really looked tired—as she'd thought about him—or that she looked a mess? Robyn asked herself silently. She managed a tight smile as she said, 'It's been a long day and this heat is wearing. They've been saying for days that the heatwave is going to break, but it hasn't happened.'

He nodded, the piercing, unrevealing stare continuing to hold her. 'The heat hit me when I stepped off the plane,' he agreed softly. 'It was cooler in the States for once.'

So he had just flown in. She ought to offer him a drink

or something. The thoughts were there but the full enormity that he was actually standing in front of her was dawning, and she didn't dare move or speak in case it revealed the trembling that was threatening to take her over.

'I know I shouldn't have come at this time of night.' He was speaking quietly, watching her face with a curious expression in his eyes that she couldn't fathom. 'But I had to, I had to try at least. If the lights hadn't been on...'

What was he talking about lights for? Why didn't he say why he was here? Was it something to do with the business? Was he going to tell her he was pulling out of their agreement now their tenuous relationship was over? The thoughts were screaming in her head but at the back of them was the realisation that she was hoping it was something else—she'd started hoping the moment she had heard his voice. Which made her the biggest idiot under the sun because, when it turned out not to be *her* he had come for, she would die all over again.

'Clay.' Her voice was croaky and she swallowed before she could try again. 'Clay, why are you here?'

'I need to explain.' And then, as though he had only just realised they were both still standing within a few feet of the door, he added, 'Do you want to go upstairs and sit down? It will take a while.'

It will take a while. She felt her senses freeze and go into cold storage. He hadn't come to say he wanted her, that he was prepared to try again, that...that he loved her. Those three words only took a second to say. But of course he hadn't, she told herself numbly. Why would he? He could have any woman he wanted so why would he come here and tell her he loved her? Oh, she was going mad here. Why couldn't he get on with it? 'No, I don't want to go upstairs,' she said on little more than a whisper, forcing the words out through stiff lips.

'Then, sit down at least.' Now he touched her for the first time and she had to nerve herself to show no emotion as she felt the warmth of his flesh on her arm as his hand guided her to her chair. She moved like a robot, stiff and unyielding.

Once she was sitting down he walked across to Drew's desk and perched on the side of it, his masculinity suddenly dwarfing the room as he looked at her with brooding eyes. 'You were right, you know.' It was husky, his accent strong for once.

'What?' She stared at him uncomprehendingly.

'Those things you said back at my house. I don't like emotion; in fact it scares the hell out of me. Emotion makes you vulnerable, open to attack, as accessible as the next man. And the most powerful emotion of them all is love. I was taught by an expert that if you love you are at your weakest, and that when the object of your love is destroyed or leaves you the pain is always with you.'

He was talking about Mitch dying, his father's gradual demise. Robyn stared at him as he looked into her eyes with an almost hypnotic intensity.

'Because I was weak, many years ago, I ran away from love into a hell of my own making,' he continued softly. 'I could have had heaven but I wasn't strong enough to reach out for it, and so for years I lied to myself. I told myself that all women were the same deep down, that betrayal and lies and heartache were the core of any relationship once you were foolish enough to trust, to love. I let someone down very badly and then I got Laura, and so to convince myself I hadn't got what I deserved I built up an armour of lies. Not a pretty picture, is it?'

He had loved a woman once? Ridiculously she felt a

stab of jealousy, the force of which tightened her hands into small fists. But why was he telling her all this? What difference did it make to them now? It was just torturing her if he did but know it.

'Robyn, do you understand what I'm saying?' His voice was low and smoky, and as she shook her head in bewilderment he rose abruptly, pacing up and down in front of her for a moment or two before he said, the words a groan, 'I'd promised myself I wouldn't touch you until I'd said it all but this is killing me.'

She gazed at him, utterly at a loss as to what was going on and then he stopped in front of her, pulling her to her feet and into his arms as he drew a long, steadying breath and ground out, 'I love you, Robyn. I've loved you for years. Loved and desired and wanted you since you were sixteen and quivered and moaned in my arms that night at the lake. There was never anyone before and there's never been anyone since, not here, in my heart.' He hit his chest with his fist.

Robyn felt the disbelief shudder through her and her face must have expressed what she was feeling because he shook her gently, his eyes wretched, before he said, 'That night at the hospital when you thought I was asleep? I heard what you said. It…it crucified me, I can't tell you.'

He had heard her? She let out a low moan of protest, of humiliation, but he crushed her against him, taking her lips in an agonised kiss as he murmured, 'Don't, oh, please, don't. It's all right; I swear I'll make it all right.'

'You…you're feeling sorry for me.' She could barely get the words out through the sobs that were shaking her. 'You don't love me, you told me you *can't* love.'

'Why do you think I've kept in touch with Guy all these years? Even after the twins were born and they reminded me of Mitch and I?'

The pain in his voice stilled her struggling but she still didn't dare let herself believe what he was saying. 'I had to know what you were doing, where you were; I couldn't get you out of my mind, Robyn. Half the time I was torturing myself with jealousy, imagining you with other men, but I still couldn't let go. That night at the lake, I would have been the first, wouldn't I? You meant what you said, about loving me?'

She nodded, unable to speak.

'I knew it deep down, even that night when I said those lies that sent you flying away from me as though I was the devil incarnate. Maybe I was,' he ground out wretchedly.

No, he hadn't been the devil, merely a terribly hurt, confused young man who hadn't dared to believe and reach out for what had seemed too good to be true to him at the time. Suddenly she understood. And because of that there had been too many wasted years, broken dreams, heartaches and vain strivings. And she had been too young herself, too much in love and too fragile to believe in herself enough to stay and talk it through.

'When I went back to the States after Cassie and Guy's wedding I was in a hell of a state,' he continued painfully, his hands stroking restlessly up and down the smooth silky skin of her arms. 'I couldn't eat, couldn't sleep; I knew then I'd made the biggest mistake of my life. The way you looked at me in those few seconds before you ran... It was eating me up inside. And so I tried to break it off with Laura.'

More things fitted into place in Robyn's whirling mind. Margo had said the state he'd been in the last few days had been mirrored once, years before, and she remembered Clay himself telling her he had tried to finish his relationship with Laura once but that she had threatened to kill herself if he didn't go through with the marriage. 'But she used emotional blackmail,' she murmured softly. 'You thought she was an innocent, shy girl who would break her heart if you let her down and broke off the engagement.'

He nodded grimly. 'But that doesn't excuse what I did to you.' Robyn could feel the turmoil shuddering through him and wondered how she could ever have considered him cold and unfeeling as she read the self-contempt and agony in his eyes.

She wanted to reach up to him, wanted to kiss away the despair in his face but all the years of suffering, the recent, raw rejection and pain, still made her just the tiniest bit unsure. She had to ask the question that was burning on her lips. 'But why, after Laura had died, didn't you come for me if you felt like that?' she asked softly, the tears still running down her face. 'I don't understand.'

'How could I?' he said harshly. 'You know the sort of man I am; how could I inflict all my hang-ups on a young, carefree girl who had the right to meet someone who could love her as she should be loved? Someone young, unsoured, someone who believed in happy ever after. But I thought of you all the time, Robyn, no matter how I tried to get you out of my mind. And I did try,' he said cynically. 'But none of them had eyes the colour of warm melted chocolate that looked at me as though I was the most wonderful thing on earth. And so I continued torturing myself, picturing you with other men, dating them, maybe loving them. And all the time living in limbo and waiting. And then Cassie called and said they were a man short for Guy's birthday party and I knew it was the moment. You deserved someone better, but it was *my* moment.'

'You...you said you wanted an affair for just a limited

time,' she reminded him dazedly. 'Right at the start you said that.'

'I told you I was a coward. You terrify me, Robyn, or rather how I feel about you terrifies me. I can't handle it. And you made it clear you were seeing me on sufferance.'

As she went to interrupt he shook her gently, saying quickly, 'Oh, I deserved it, I knew I deserved it, but from the moment I saw you again I knew I couldn't let you go, and there you were—so icy cold, looking at me as though I was something you'd found under a stone. But Cassie had given me the perfect excuse to stay in your life and I intended to use it.'

'The sleeping partner.' Oh, Cass, Cass.

'And I thought, okay, so that night all those years ago meant nothing to you now and you were never going to love me like I knew I loved you, but you did *want* me, physically. It was something.'

'And so the self-protection of a lifetime came into place,' she murmured softly. 'Oh, Clay.'

'But you were strong, so strong: giving out the dictates, setting out the rules. Hell, no one had ever done that to me before.' His voice carried a note of absolute amazement. 'And so I told myself I'd wear you down and then for however long you stayed with me we'd enjoy each other. But each day I loved you more and whatever I did or said you held me at arm's length. Your power over me scared me to death. You seemed to read my mind, know exactly what made me tick.'

'But I felt that about *you*.' She was gazing at him in amazed wonder. 'All along I thought you were doing that.'

'You destroyed me that night at the house before we went to the hospital,' he said slowly, 'and then, when you came to stand at the side of me and said what you did...I couldn't take it in at first. I can't remember hardly anything after that, even the baby.'

She remembered the look on his face when she had seen him in the delivery room, the look she had attributed to his wonder at seeing Samantha, and for the first time she recognised the disbelief that had been mixed up with the stunned incredulity.

'I had to get away, sort it out in my mind; I owed you that,' he said painfully. 'I had to be sure that all those demons you spoke about had gone and that I could offer you my trust as well as my love, and then the decision would be yours. It *is* yours. I have no right to ask you to continue to love me or stay with me and if you want me to get out of your life—' He stopped abruptly, his head jerking up as he took a steadying breath. 'Well, I'll try but being the man I am I can't promise I won't come back.'

And now Robyn did what she had been longing to do: she reached up her hands to cradle his face, bringing his lips down to hers and for the second time in her life she kissed him first.

For a moment he was still and she could feel his heart thundering against his ribcage as she pressed herself against the hard bulk of him, and then he whispered her name in an agonised groan against her mouth, kissing her with a hunger that she met all the way.

There was a starving quality to his kisses as he covered her face and her throat before returning to her lips which were open and yielding to his mouth, and he was crushing her to him in his desire until she felt her bones would snap. But she didn't try to move away even the slightest, knowing he was still needing reassurance, that he would probably continue to need it for a long time. But she didn't mind that now he was hers.

And then he seemed to come to himself, tearing his lips

from hers and taking long, ragged breaths as he fought for control, before he said, 'I'm hurting you. Hell, after everything else I'm hurting you.'

'No, no.' She was so euphoric and drunk with love that she didn't care. He loved her. *He loved her.* And she sensed now that Margo, loving him as she did, had known all along.

'I love you, Robyn. I'll tell you every minute of every day until you're sick of hearing it,' he said brokenly. 'I want to marry you; I want you to be my wife. I want to fill our home with children and cats and dogs and anything else that speaks of commitment and for ever and happy ever after, but most of all I want you. I'll regret to my dying day I didn't take what you so sweetly offered all those years ago, but I'll make it up to you, my darling. I promise. I'll love you like no one else has or could.'

She looked at him, her heart full with the gift she could give him. The gift that—with his tortured childhood and dark memories of his mother—she knew would mean something precious. 'There hasn't been anyone else, Clay,' she said softly. 'Not emotionally or physically. You will be the first and the last, my only love. How could I have given myself to anyone else? You were the one Cass spoke about without knowing it was you.'

He just looked at her, his love blazing from eyes that were suddenly wet, and then their mouths met in a kiss that was deep and timeless, a kiss that reached into eternity and back. A kiss that sealed their future more surely than any gold wedding band.

'For ever, sweetheart?' He raised his head and looked down into her face, seeing the adoration there with a thankfulness that reached to the depths of his heart.

'For ever.' And she clung to him, her eyes wide and shining as she reached up for his lips again, and then there was no need for further words...

EPILOGUE

As THE doors to the maternity unit swung open the quiet serenity of the hospital was suddenly shattered by the sound of a very deep and authoritative male voice shouting orders.

Sister Robinson raised her head and listened from the sanctity of her little office, but when the rumpus without showed no signs of abating she rose to her feet, her homely face frowning. Who on earth was upsetting her nice, orderly unit like this? she asked herself grimly, smoothing down her starched uniform and checking her cap was in place as she looked in the mirror, her eyes holding a distinctly steely glint as she swept out of the door.

She came to a halt in the reception to see a tall, lean dark-haired man who was standing with his back to her, his arm protectively enclosing a very pregnant, red-haired woman who was saying quietly, 'But I really don't want a wheelchair, darling. I'm more than capable of walking.'

'Is there a problem?' The good sister's voice was of a quality that brought all eyes facing her way, and as she looked at the man in front of her she closed her eyes for an infinitesimal moment before saying resignedly, 'Mr Lincoln.'

'Sister Robinson.' Clay beamed at the reassuring sight of the large, middle-aged and supremely capable nurse. 'You remember me!'

'Oh, yes, Mr Lincoln. I remember you,' Sister Robinson said with some feeling.

'My wife is having a baby,' Clay said agitatedly.

'Then, she is in the right place, isn't she, Mr Lincoln?'

'You don't understand, Sister. It's coming *now*.'

'Don't worry, Mr Lincoln,' the sister said soothingly before she turned to one of the nurses saying, 'I'll deal with Mrs Lincoln, nurse. We'll use room three. Now, Mr Lincoln, why don't you go and get a nice cup of coffee while we settle your wife into bed and then you can come and hold her hand. I presume you want to stay with her during the birth?'

'Of course I do.' Clay looked at her as though she was mad to even suggest anything else. 'But—'

'No buts, Mr Lincoln.'

Sister Robinson had her arm around Robyn and was about to lead her away when Clay opened his mouth to say more. The sister fixed him with her gimlet eyes for a moment and as his mouth shut with a little snap said reassuringly over her shoulder, 'We won't be a minute, Mr Lincoln.'

Robyn was giggling as the sister led her into the delivery room. 'You haven't seen him at his best, Sister,' she said on a hiccup of a laugh. 'He's normally the most controlled, capable, unflappable man in the world.'

Sister Robinson smiled back. 'I'll take your word for it, Mrs Lincoln,' she said briskly. 'Now, let's get you dressed and into bed...'

Five hours later Robyn and Clay's son made his way into the world and he was a big, healthy baby with a shock of jet-black hair and slate-blue eyes. His father wept unashamedly as he held him in his arms, and Clay's face, as he gazed at his wife, brought a lump to the midwife's and Sister Robinson's throat, the latter having popped in on her way off duty.

'Have you a name for baby?' the sister asked Robyn, her voice a little choked.

'Daniel Mitchell, after my husband's father and brother,' Robyn said softly, reaching up and stroking Clay's face as he sat beside her on the bed.

'That's nice,' Sister Robinson said comfortably as she bustled out of the room. 'I'll see you tomorrow, Mrs Lincoln, and I suppose you'll be here, Mr Lincoln?' she added with a faint, teasing note.

'Oh, yes, Sister, I'll be here,' Clay replied without taking his eyes off Robyn's tired, beautiful face, the baby cradled in his arms yawning sleepily as the sister shut the door.

It was so *nice* to meet a man like Mr Lincoln, the sister reflected as she drove home a few minutes later, the radiant little scene in the hospital room staying with her. A man who wasn't afraid to show his emotions...

The world's bestselling romance series.

HARLEQUIN®
Presents

Seduction and Passion Guaranteed!

VIVA LA VIDA DE AMOR!

They speak the language of passion.

In Harlequin Presents®, you'll find a special kind of
lover—full of Latin charm. Whether he's relaxing in
denims, or dressed for dinner, giving you diamonds, or
simply sweet dreams, he's got spirit, style and sex appeal!

Look out for our next Latin Lovers titles:

A SPANISH INHERITANCE by Susan Stephens
#2318, on sale April 2003

ALEJANDRO'S REVENGE by Anne Mather
#2327, on sale June 2003

Available wherever Harlequin books are sold.

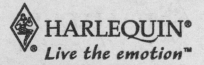

HARLEQUIN®
Live the emotion™

Visit us at www.eHarlequin.com

HPLATMAR

The world's bestselling romance series.

HARLEQUIN®
Presents~

Seduction and Passion Guaranteed!

**Anything can happen
behind closed doors!
Do you dare find out…?**

Meet Crystal and Sam, a couple
thrown together by circumstances
into a whirlwind of unexpected
attraction. Forced into each other's
company whether they like it or
not, they're soon in the grip of
passion—and definitely *don't*
want to be disturbed!

**Popular Harlequin Presents®
author Carole Mortimer explores
this delicious fantasy in a
tantalizing romance you simply
won't want to put down.**

AN ENIGMATIC MAN
#2316
April on-sale

Available wherever Harlequin books are sold.

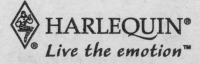

HARLEQUIN®
Live the emotion™

Visit us at www.eHarlequin.com

HPDNDIS

eHARLEQUIN.com

Calling all aspiring writers!
Learn to craft the perfect romance novel
with our useful tips and tools:

- Take advantage of our **Romance Novel Critique Service** for detailed advice from romance professionals.

- Use our **message boards** to connect with writers, published authors and editors.

- Enter our **Writing Round Robin—** you could be published online!

- Learn many writing hints in our **Top 10 Writing lists!**

- **Guidelines** for Harlequin or Silhouette novels—what our editors *really* look for.

Learn more about romance writing from the experts—

visit www.eHarlequin.com today!

INTLTW

HARLEQUIN®

AMERICAN *Romance®*

Celebrate 20 Years
of Home, Heart and Happiness!

Join us for a yearlong anniversary celebration as we
bring you not-to-be-missed miniseries such as:

MILLIONAIRE, MONTANA

A small town wins a huge jackpot in this six-book continuity
(January–June 2003)

THE BABIES OF DOCTORS CIRCLE

Jacqueline Diamond's darling doctor trilogy
(March, May, July 2003)

A ROYAL TWIST

Victoria Chancellor's witty royal duo
(January and February 2003)

And look for your favorite authors throughout the year, including:

Muriel Jensen's JACKPOT BABY (January 2003)

Judy Christenberry's
SAVED BY A TEXAS-SIZED WEDDING (May 2003)

Cathy Gillen Thacker's brand-new
DEVERAUX LEGACY story (June 2003)

Look for more exciting programs throughout the year
as Harlequin American Romance celebrates its 20th Anniversary!

Available at your favorite retail outlet.

 **HARLEQUIN®**
Makes any time special®

Visit us at www.eHarlequin.com   HARTAC

A "Mother of the Year" contest brings overwhelming response as thousands of women vie for the luxurious grand prize....

Kate Hoffmann

Jacqueline Diamond

Jill Shalvis

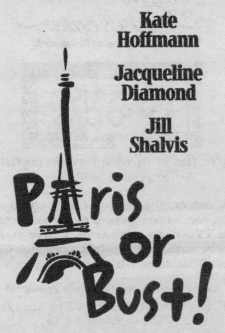

Paris or Bust!

A hilarious and romantic trio of new stories!

With a trip to Paris at stake, these women are determined to win! But the laughs are many as three of them discover that being finalists isn't the most excitement they'll ever have…. Falling in love is!

Available in April 2003.

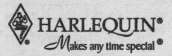

HARLEQUIN®
Makes any time special ®

Visit us at www.eHarlequin.com

PHPOB

The world's bestselling romance series.

HARLEQUIN®
Presents

Seduction and Passion Guaranteed!

GREEK TYCOONS

They're the men who have everything—except a bride...

Wealth, power, charm—what else could a heart-stopping handsome tycoon need? Find out in the GREEK TYCOONS miniseries, where your very favorite authors introduce gorgeous Greek multimillionaires who are in need of wives!

Coming soon in Harlequin Presents®

SMOKESCREEN MARRIAGE by Sara Craven
#2320, on sale May 2003

THE GREEK TYCOON'S BRIDE by Helen Brooks
#2328, on sale June 2003

THE GREEK'S SECRET PASSION by Sharon Kendrick
#2339, on sale August 2003

Available wherever Harlequin books are sold.

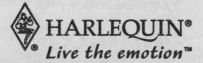

HARLEQUIN®
Live the emotion™

Visit us at www.eHarlequin.com

HPGTYC